P9-CBK-765

THE AUTHOR: Yukio Mishima, one of the most spectacularly gifted writers in modern Japan, was born into a samurai family in 1925. He attended the Peers' School and Tokyo Imperial University, and for a time worked at the Ministry of Finance. His first full-length novel, *Confessions of a Mask*, appeared in 1949, and since then he published over a dozen novels, almost all of which were translated into English and other languages during his lifetime. They include: *Thirst for Love; Forbidden Colors; Death in Mid-summer; The Sound of Waves; The Temple of the Golden Pavilion; After the Banquet; The Sailor Who Fell from Grace with the Sea;* and *Spring Snow*.

Mishima's reverence for the Japanese martial arts led him to take up Kendo (a type of fencing, with wooden swords) and Karate, as well as body-building, and by 1968 he had become a Kendo master of the fifth *dan*. He also organized a "private army" called the Shield Society, and in November 1970 he and his group forced their way into a Self-Defense Force headquarters in Tokyo, where Mishima, after reading out a proclamation, committed ritual suicide with a young follower in the commanding officer's room. On the morning of his death, the last volume of Mishima's tetralogy, *The Sea of Fertility*, was delivered to his publisher.

He is survived by his wife and two children.

THE TRANSLATOR: John Bester, born and educated in England, is one of the foremost translators of Japanese fiction. Among his translations are Masuji Ibuse's *Black Rain*, Kenzaburo Oe's *The Silent Cry*, Fumiko Enchi's *The Waiting Years*, Junnosuke Yoshiyuki's *The Dark Room*, and Mishima's autobiographical *Sun and Steel*. He received the 1990 Noma Award for the Translation of Japanese Literature (for *Acts of Worship*).

ACTS OF WORSHIP

Seven Stories

YUKIO MISHIMA

Translated by John Bester

KODANSHA INTERNATIONAL
Tokyo and New York

The original titles of "Fountains in the Rain," "Raisin Bread," "Sword," "Sea and Sunset," "Cigarette," "Martyrdom," and "Act of Worship" are respectively: *Ame no naka no funsui*; *Budopan*; *Ken*; *Umi to yuyake*; *Tabako*; *Junkyo*; and *Mikumano mode*.

Distributed in the United States by Kodansha International/ USA Ltd., 114 Fifth Avenue, New York, NY 10011. Published by Kodansha International Ltd., 17-14, Otowa 1-chome, Bunkyo-ku, Tokyo 112 and Kodansha International/USA Ltd. This anthology copyright © 1989 by Kodansha International. Individual stories (*Tabako*, 1946; *Junkyo*, 1948; *Umi to yuyake*, 1955; *Ken*, *Ame no naka no funsui*, *Budopan*, 1963; *Mikumano mode*, 1965) © Yoko Mishima. All rights reserved. Printed in Japan.
LCC 89-45171
ISBN 0-87011-824-2 (U.S.)
ISBN 4-7700-1507-0 (Japan)
First edition, 1989
First paperback edition, 1990

CONTENTS

PREFACE

Twenty years on, it is time for a reappraisal of Mishima: time to strip his reputation of any accretions arising from sensationalism, chic, or special interest and to take a cool look at his work as world literature.

The faults are readily apparent: a certain restriction of theme; an evident self-indulgence at times; lapses of an undeniable brilliance into cleverness, if not bad taste. These are not, in moderation, fatal; the case of D. H. Lawrence comes to mind. What is more important is whether Mishima, as D. H. Lawrence does, uses his particular preoccupations to create real worlds from which universal (which does not necessarily mean immediately familiar to the Western reader) themes transpire. At the very least—and this matters particularly in a selection of short stories—does he create forms sufficiently well wrought, or of a sufficiently compelling symbolism, to satisfy irrespective of their content?

With the present selection of stories, which extends over a large part of Mishima's career, the answer in both cases is, I feel, a definite yes. The close acquaintance that the task of translation entails has convinced me that Mishima here is often at his very best. The sheer power of organization, and the ability to suggest various levels that present themselves with rereading, is undeniable, especially in the later stories. Equally undeniable is the beauty of the imagery, and his gift for endowing a story with its own unmistakable atmosphere and coloring. More unexpected in Mishima is a power, from time to time, to move.

The ability to organize a small form is very evident in "Fountains in the Rain." A slight, humorous account of a tiff between a very ordinary young man and his girl, it skillfully portrays the instability, lack of confidence, and above all the self centeredness that often characterize youth. With great skill, the imagery set forth in the title is worked into the fabric of the story; in a central set piece of description, the fountains reveal themselves as a symbol of the shifting impulses—ambition, aggression, sexuality—to which the hero is prey, and which are liable at any moment to be negated by the monotony of every day life—the rain—and its obligations. The girl is barely sketched in, but the suggestion of a firmer grasp of immediate realities provides a good foil to the boy's instability.

More ambitious perhaps in its semi-surrealist effects, "Raisin Bread" portrays a group of young people of the fifties (a real group, whose friendliness to Mishima is gracefully acknowledged by him in a note to the story) making a pathetic and by now hopelessly old-fashioned protest against society. At their center stands the figure of Jack, a young man in full retreat from the world and himself, obsessed with non-involvement yet with a touch of sentimental idealism, a failed suicide who reaches out in self-disgust for the other oblivion of sexuality.

"Sword," with its muscles, its sweat, and its amber flesh, might seem at a casual glance to be the most self-indulgent of all the stories here. In fact, it is the reverse, and a close study only increases one's respect for Mishima's powers of detached observation. It also reveals most clearly the ability to suggest various layers of meaning that I have referred to above.

First and most obviously, the story is a picture of the world of college *kendo*—Japanese fencing—a world characterized here by oppressively oversensitive personal relations and an immature hero worship that leads indirectly to disaster. It is notable, though, that the hero worship does not come from the author, who is remarkably clear-eyed about his main character's priggishness. He even, with unusual explicitness, provides the clue to Jiro's behavior in a short passage describing his family background. Given that background, everything about Jiro—the preoccupation with uprightness, the remoteness from sexuality, the reluctance to enter ordinary social life—is readily understandable in psychological terms.

This indicates the second way in which the story functions: as a psychological study of a young man trying to deny his father and be self-sufficient, a young man in whom the inevitable weakness that culminates in tragedy is not offset by any artistic sensibility—the "poetry" of the pigeon episode—such as might have offered salvation.

But there is a third level too, at which Mishima reexamines a favorite theme: the relationship between pure "being" and intellectual apprehension, between the unselfconscious certainties of animal existence and the cluttered ambiguities of everyday life. There is an obvious link with Zen here, a link that is skillfully hinted at when he sets the second (and, I feel, more successful) part of the story in a Buddhist temple; in this setting, the poetic and metaphysical purpose of the muscles and the amber skin—of the beautiful, unreflecting forces and surfaces—becomes clear. The story, like the later "Act of Worship," achieves a striking consistency of coloring and atmosphere.

"Sea and Sunset" is a relatively straightforward and deeply romantic little fable. The side of Mishima that rejects Western civilization, with its impossibly ambitious view of humanity and its self-deceptions, is here balanced by a sense of regret at the need to reject that civilization, and by a nostalgic admiration for its achievements. It is surely no accident that he paints his picture with the simplicity and glowing primary colors of an early Renaissance painting.

"Cigarette," the work that first won Mishima attention in the literary world, is a sensitive study of a bookish, sheltered youth on the threshold of sexuality and the search for love outside the family. The story begins in a rather self-consciously "literary" way which is more than made up for later by its extremely delicate human insight. This never becomes crudely explicit, being revealed solely through a series of poetic images; yet after careful reading one could, if one wished, explain what is happening to the chief character in the most detailed and convincing psychological terms. Particularly subtle is the exchange between that character and Imura that takes place near the end of the story. Here, Mishima brilliantly suggests how the desperate desire for identification with the love object is matched by an even more desperate desire—sadly, in the event, betrayed—to be rescued from the claims of sexuality by love. (It is a measure of the story's delicacy that even this account seems crude.) As a whole, the narrative seems to me to achieve a poignancy that far transcends the narrowly homoerotic aspects of the theme.

The roughly contemporary "Martyrdom" has obvious affinities with "Cigarette." Perhaps more contrived, it is certainly more enigmatic. In notes for the story, Mishima refers to Watari as "the Poet," so the relationship between the two boys is possibly meant to symbolize the relationship between the artist and the man of action. Either way, the piece surely succeeds on the strength of its striking, perverted poetry alone.

That the "Professor" in "Act of Worship" was clearly modeled on a well-known scholar of the day is irrelevant to the finished work of art. Despite the initial unattractiveness of the two central characters, the story, far from being malicious, is ultimately the most moving of this selection in its compassionate recognition of the unlikely ways in which human beings fulfill each other's emotional needs. It is also brilliantly organized, and repays frequent rereading.

It works, first of all, purely as a story, depending for its interest on the central puzzle of the Professor's motives. The contemporary action is skillfully interwoven with discursions into the medieval world of literature and political intrigue, thus giving conviction to the accounts of the Professor's studies and variety to the pace of the narrative. The frequent references to, and actual quotations from, the poetry of Eifuku Mon'in point up the short passages of natural description, which—surely consciously—are given the gloss and subtle suggestiveness of the poet's own work. The Nachi waterfall, with its many different aspects, and the descriptions of the Kumano area, have an obviously symbolic bearing on the main characters. And the whole story has a characteristic interplay of surfaces, colors, and effects of light that gives it a quality as distinctive as, yet quite different from, that of "Sword." Working on the story had already convinced me of its very special qualities when I happened to learn that Mishima himself was particularly proud of it.

The relative lack of attention paid to Mishima in Japan at the moment is almost certainly due in part to embarrassment or disgust at the manner of his death. It may also be accounted for by his style. This has at times, alongside its brilliance, an undoubted difficulty and also a certain hardness of texture which, to some Japanese readers, may seem rebarbative, while its occasional mannerisms are too recent to be either beyond parody or sanctioned by time. Mishima's profundities, moreover, are of a kind that requires more purely intellectual effort to perceive than the profundities of pure sensibility characterizing much of Japanese literature. None of these factors should affect Mishima's reputation in the long run.

I have taken few conscious liberties with the texts. In "Raisin Bread," the characters use a slang that involves reversing the two halves of some nouns (*naon* for *onna*, "woman," etc.). It is a purely mechanical trick conveying—I am told—no special atmosphere, and is entirely outdated, so I judged it better not to attempt anything similar in English. There are a few short passages that I have cut because they would have been impossible to translate, or would have been puzzling to the non-Japanese reader. They amount to a total of a dozen lines or so over the whole book; elsewhere, I have tried to render the original as faithfully as possible.

John Bester

N.B. Japanese names in the stories follow the Japanese order—family name first.

FOUNTAINS
IN
THE RAIN

The boy was tired of walking in the rain dragging the girl, heavy as a sandbag and weeping continually, around with him.

A short while ago, in a tea shop in the Marunouchi Building, he had told her he was leaving her.

The first time in his life that he'd broken with a woman!

It was something he had long dreamed of; it had at last become a reality.

It was for this alone that he had loved her, or pretended to love her; for this alone he had assiduously undermined her defenses; for this alone he'd furiously sought the chance to sleep with her, slept with her—till lo, the preparations were complete and it only remained to pronounce the phrase he had longed just once to pronounce with his own lips, with due authority, like the edict of a king:

"It's time to break it off!"

Those words, the mere enunciation of which would be enough to rend the sky asunder. . . . Those words that he had cherished so passionately even while half-resigned to the impossibility of the fact. . . . That phrase, more heroic, more glorious than any other in the world, which would fly in a straight line through the heavens like an arrow released from its bow. . . . That spell which only the most human of humans, the most manly of men, might utter. . . . In short:

"It's time to break it off!"

All the same, Akio felt a lingering regret that he'd been obliged to say it with such a deplorable lack of clarity, with a rattling noise in the throat, like an asthmatic with a throatful of phlegm, which even a preliminary draft of soda pop through his straw had failed to avert.

At the time, his chief fear had been that the words might not have been heard. He'd have died sooner than be asked what he'd said and have to repeat it. After all, if a goose that for years had longed to lay a golden egg had found it smashed before anyone could see it, would it promptly have laid another?

Fortunately, however, she had heard. She'd heard, and he hadn't had to repeat it, which was a splendid piece of luck. Under his own steam, Akio had crossed the pass over the mountains that he'd gazed at for so long in the distance.

Sure proof that she'd heard had been vouchsafed in a flash, like chewing gum ejected from a vending machine.

The windows were closed because of the rain, so that the voices of the customers talking around them, the clatter of dishes, the ping of the cash register clashed with each other all the more violently, rebounding subtly off the clammy condensation on the inside of the panes to create a single, mind-fuddling commotion.

Akio's muffled words had no sooner reached Masako's ears through the general uproar than her eyes—wide, staring eyes that seemed to be trying to shove her surroundings away from her thin, unprepossessing features—opened still wider. They were no longer eyes so much as an embodiment of disaster, irretrievable disaster. And then, all at once, the tears had burst forth.

There was no business of breaking into sobs; nor did she bawl her head off: the tears simply gushed, expressing nothing, and with a most impressive force.

Akio naturally assumed that waters of such pressure and flow

4

would soon cease. And he marveled at the peppermint freshness of mind with which he contemplated the phenomenon. This was precisely what he had planned, worked to encompass, and brought to reality: a splendid achievement, though admittedly somewhat mechanical.

It was to witness this, he told himself again, that he had made love to Masako: he, who had always been free from the dominance of desire.

And the tearful face of the woman now in front of him—this was reality! A genuine forsaken woman—forsaken by himself, Akio!

Even so, Masako's tears went on for so long with no sign of abating that the boy began to worry about the people around them.

Masako, still wearing her light-colored raincoat, was sitting upright in her chair. The collar of a red blouse showed at the neck of the coat. She looked as though set in her present position, with her hands pressed down on the edge of the table, a tremendous force in both of them.

She stared straight ahead, letting the tears flow unchecked. She made no move to take out a handkerchief to wipe them. Her breath, catching in her thin throat, gave out a regular wheeze like new shoes, and the mouth that with student perverseness she refused to paint turned up disconsolately, quivering continually.

The older customers were looking at them curiously, with stares of a kind calculated to disturb Akio's newfound sense of maturity.

The abundance of Masako's tears was a genuine cause for astonishment. Not for a moment did their volume diminish. Tired of watching, Akio dropped his gaze and looked at the tip of the umbrella he had stood against a chair. The raindrops run-

5

ning from it had formed a small, darkish puddle on the old-fashioned, tile mosaic floor. Even the puddle began to look like Masako's tears to him.

Abruptly, he grabbed the bill and stood up.

The June rains had been falling steadily for three days. As he left the Marunouchi Building and unfurled his umbrella, the girl came silently after him. Since she had no umbrella herself, he had no choice but to let her share his. It reminded him of the way older people, for the benefit of the outside world, went on pretending even after they'd stopped feeling anything. Now he too had acquired the same habit; to share an umbrella with a girl once you'd made the move to break with her was just a gesture for other people's benefit. It was simply being cut-and-dried about things. Yes: to be cut-and-dried (even when it took such subtle forms) suited Akio's nature. . . .

As they wandered along the broad sidewalk in the direction of the Imperial Palace, the problem foremost in his mind was finding somewhere to dump this tearbag he was saddled with.

I wonder—he thought vaguely to himself—if the fountains work even when it's raining?

Why should the idea of fountains have occurred to him? Another few paces, and he realized the physical pun in his own train of thought.

The girl's wet raincoat, which he was touching—remotely, of course, and unfeelingly—in the cramped space beneath the umbrella, had the texture of a reptile. But he bore with it, forcing his mind to follow the pun to its logical conclusion.

Yes: fountains in the rain. He'd bring the fountains and Masako's tears into confrontation. Even Masako would surely find her match there. For one thing, the fountains were the type that used the same water over and over again, so the girl, whose tears all ran to waste, could hardly compete with them. A human being was scarcely a match for a reflex fountain; almost certainly, she'd give up and stop crying. Then he'd be able somehow to get rid of this unwanted baggage. The only question was whether the fountains would be working as usual in the rain.

Akio walked in silence. Masako, still weeping, followed doggedly under the same umbrella. Thus, while it was difficult to shake her off, it was easy to drag her along where he wanted.

What with the rain and the tears, Akio felt as if his whole body was getting wet. It was all right for Masako in her white boots, but his own socks, inside his loafers, felt like thick, wet seaweed around his feet.

There was some time still before the office workers came out, and the sidewalk was deserted. Traversing a pedestrian crossing, they made their way toward Wadakura Bridge, which crossed the palace moat. When they reached the end of the bridge with its old-fashioned wooden railings topped by pointed knobs, they could see on their left a swan floating on the moat in the rain and, to the right, on the other side of the moat, the white tablecloths and red chairs of a hotel dining room, dimly visible through rain-blurred glass. They crossed the bridge. Passing between high stone ramparts, they turned left and emerged in the small garden with the fountains.

Masako, as ever, was crying soundlessly.

Just inside the garden was a large Western-style summerhouse. The benches under its roof, which consisted of a kind of blind of fine reeds, were protected to some extent from the rain, so Akio sat down with his umbrella still up and Masako sat down next to him, at an angle, so that all he could see, right in front of his nose, was a shoulder of her white raincoat and her wet hair. The rain on the hair, repelled by the oil on it, looked like a scattering of fine white dew. Still crying, with her eyes wide open, she might almost have been in some kind of coma, and Akio felt an urge to give the hair a tug, to bring her out of it.

She went on crying, endlessly. It was perfectly clear that she was waiting for him to say something, which made it impossible, as a matter of pride, for him to break the silence. It occurred to him that since that one momentous sentence he hadn't spoken a single word.

Not far away, the fountains were throwing up their waters in profusion, but Masako showed no inclination to look at them.

Seen from here, head on, the three fountains, two small and one large, were lined up one behind the other, and the sound, blotted out by the rain, was distant and faint, but the fact that their blurring of spray was not visible at a distance gave the lines of water, dividing up in various directions, a clearly defined look like curved glass tubes.

Not a soul was in sight anywhere. The lawn on this side of the fountains and the low ornamental hedge were a brilliant green in the rain.

Beyond the garden, though, there was a constant procession of wet truck hoods and bus roofs in red, white, or yellow; the red light of a signal at a crossing was clearly visible, but when it changed to the lower green, the light disappeared in a cloud of spray from the fountains.

The act of sitting down and remaining still and silent aroused an indefinable anger in the boy. With it, amusement at his little joke of a while ago disappeared.

He couldn't have said what he was angry about. Not long before, he had been on a kind of high, but now, suddenly, he was beset with an obscure sense of dissatisfaction. Nor was his inability to dispose of the forever crying Masako the whole extent of the frustration.

Her? I could easily deal with *her* if I cared to, he told himself. I could just shove her in the fountain and do a bunk—and that would be the end of it. The thought restored his earlier elation. No, the only trouble was the absolute frustration he felt at the rain, the tears, the leaden sky that hung like a barrier before him. They pressed down on him on all sides, reducing his freedom to a kind of damp rag.

Angry, the boy gave in to a simple desire to hurt. Nothing would satisfy him now till he had got Masako thoroughly soaked in the rain and given her a good eyeful of the fountains.

Getting up suddenly, he set off running without so much as a glance back; raced on along the gravel path that encircled the fountains outside and a few steps higher than the walk around the fountains themselves; reached a spot that gave a full view of them; and came to a halt.

The girl came running through the rain. Checking herself just as she was about to collide with him, she took a firm grip of the umbrella he was holding up. Damp with tears and rain, her face was pale.

"Where are you going?" she said through her gasps.

Akio was not supposed to reply, yet found himself talking as effortlessly as though he'd been waiting for her to ask this very thing.

"Just look at the fountains. Look! You can cry as much as you like, but you're no match for *them*."

And the two of them tilted the umbrella and, freed from the need to keep their eyes on each other, stared for a while at the three fountains: the central one imposing, the other two slighter, like attendants flanking it on both sides.

Amidst the constant turmoil of the fountains and the pool around them, the streaks of rain falling into the water were almost indistinguishable. Paradoxically, the only sound that

9

struck the ear was the fitful drone of distant cars; the noise of the fountains wove itself so closely into the surrounding air that unless you made an effort to hear you seemed to be enclosed in perfect silence.

First, the water at the bottom bounced in isolated drops off the huge shallow basin of black granite, then ran in a continual drizzle over the black rim.

Another six jets of water, describing far-flung radiating arcs in the air, stood guard around the main column that shot upward from the center of each basin.

This column, if you watched carefully, did not always achieve the same height. In the almost complete absence of a breeze, the water spouted vertically and undisturbed toward the gray, rainy sky, varying from time to time in the height of its summit. Occasionally, ragged water would be flung up to an astonishing height before finally dispersing into droplets and floating to earth again.

The water near the summit, shadowed by the clouds that were visible through it, was gray with an admixture of chalky white, almost too powdery-looking for real water, and a misty spray clung about it, while around the column played a mass of foam in large white flakes mingling like snow with the rain.

But Akio was less taken with the three main columns of water than with the water that shot out in radiating curves all around.

The jets from the big central fountain in particular leaped far above the marble rim, flinging up their white manes only to dash themselves gallantly down again onto the surface of the pool. The sight of their untiring rushing to the four quarters threatened to usurp his attention. Almost before he knew it, his mind, which till now had been with him in this place, was being taken over by the water, carried away on its rushing, cast far away. . . .

It was the same when he watched the central column.

At first glance, it seemed as neat, as motionless, as a sculpture fashioned out of water. Yet watching closely he could see a transparent ghost of movement moving upward from bottom to top. With furious speed it climbed, steadily filling a slender cylinder of space from base to summit, replacing each moment what had been lost the moment before, in a kind of perpetual replenishment. It was plain that at heaven's height it would be finally frustrated; yet the unwaning power that supported unceasing failure was magnificent.

The fountains he had brought the girl to see had ended by completely fascinating the boy himself. He was still dwelling on their virtues when his gaze, lifted higher, met the sky from which the all-enveloping rain was falling.

He got rain on his eyelashes.

The sky, hemmed in by dense clouds, hung low over his head; the rain fell copiously and without cease. The whole scene was filled with rain. The rain descending on his face was exactly the same as that falling on the roofs of the red-brick buildings and hotel in the distance. His own almost beardless face, smooth and shiny, and the rough concrete that floored the deserted roof of one of those buildings were no more than two surfaces exposed, unresisting, to the same rain. From the rain's point of view, his cheeks and the dirty concrete roof were quite identical.

Immediately, the image of the fountains there before his eyes was wiped from his mind. Quite suddenly, fountains in the rain seemed to represent no more than the endless repetition of a stupid and pointless process.

Before long, he had forgotten both his joke of a while ago and the anger that had followed it, and felt his mind steadily becoming empty.

Empty, save for the falling rain. . . .

Aimlessly, the boy started walking.

"Where are you going?" She fell into step with him as she spoke, this time keeping a firm hold on the handle of the umbrella.

"Where? That's my business, isn't it? I told you quite plainly some time ago, didn't I?"

"What did you tell me?"

He gazed at her in horror, but the rain had washed away the traces of tears from the drenched face, and although the damp, reddened eyes still showed the aftermath of weeping, the voice in which she spoke was no longer shaky.

"What do you mean, 'what'? I told you a while back, didn't I?—that we'd better split up."

Just then, the boy spotted, beyond her profile as it moved through the rain, some crimson azalea bushes blooming, small and grudgingly, here and there on the lawn.

"Really? Did you say that? I didn't hear you." Her voice was normal.

Almost bowled over by shock, the boy managed a few steps further before an answer finally came and he stammered:

"But—in that case, what did you cry for? I don't get it."

She didn't reply immediately. Her wet little hand was still firmly attached to the umbrella handle.

"The tears just came. There wasn't any special reason."

Furious, he wanted to shout something at her, but at the crucial moment it came out as an enormous sneeze.

If I'm not careful I'm going to get a cold, he thought.

RAISIN
BREAD

Turning inland at eleven-thirty on an August night with his back to the white grinding of the waves on the beach, Jack began to climb the broad, sandy cutting that ran up beside the Yuigahama Hotel.

He had made it somehow from Tokyo by hitching rides. As a result, it was a good deal later than the time he'd been supposed to meet up with Peter and Keeko, in addition to which the truck had dropped him off at the wrong spot. But you could get to the meeting place this way too, though it was a long detour, and much farther to walk.

Peter, the girl, and the rest of them would have given him up long ago and gone straight on to the rendezvous.

Jack, twenty-two and made of some clear crystalline substance, had as his sole aim to become quite invisible.

Something of an expert in English, a translator in his spare time of science fiction stories, with a past that included an attempted suicide, he was slim, with a good face fashioned of ivory. It was the kind of face you could strike repeatedly without provoking any response; so no one ever struck it.

Someone in the modern jazz cafe had summed him up by saying that if you took a running jump at him, you'd find you'd gone straight through and out the other side. . . .

The banks of the cutting loomed on either hand. Few stars were out; as he ascended the slope, the beating of the waves behind him and the roar of cars on the tollroad faded into the distance, and a dense silence took over everything. The sand ran off the insteps of his feet, bare in their rubber sandals.

Someone, somewhere, had tied up the darkness, he thought as he went: the bag of darkness had been tied at the mouth, enclosing within it a host of smaller bags. The stars were tiny, almost imperceptible perforations; otherwise, there wasn't a single hole through which light could pass.

The darkness in which he walked immersed was gradually pervading him. His own footfall was utterly remote, his presence barely rippled the air. His being had been compressed to the utmost—to the point where it had no need to forge a path for itself through the night, but could weave its way through the gaps between the particles of which the darkness was composed.

To become transparent, to be free of all things, Jack retained nothing unnecessary: no muscles, no fat, only a beating heart and the idea, like a white sugared candy, of an "angel"....

All of which was probably the effect of barbiturates. Before leaving his apartment, he'd taken five of them in a glass of beer.

The slope whose top he reached before long opened onto a spacious tableland, on the other side of which he saw two cars squatting on the firm sand like discarded shoes.

Jack broke into a run. "Running!" he reflected, pursuing himself in dismay. "Me, running! . . ."

The broad path led to the far side of the plateau, which abruptly fell away to a deep gully on whose floor lay a pool of still denser darkness. Suddenly, Jack saw smooth flames flickering upward. It was as though the night, with a loud noise, were starting to disintegrate from that one point, just as a whole embankment begins to burst from one small hole.

Trampling through the dry undergrowth, Jack slipped and slid as he ran down sand that might or might not be a path, heading for the bottom of the gully. He felt rather like a fly slipping down into a sugar basin.

The confusion of human sounds at the bottom came closer, but with another twist in the interior of the gorge the great flames he had seen moments earlier vanished, and the voices came closer to hand, though still no human forms were visible. The stones beneath his feet grew more numerous; as in a dream, they would suddenly rear up, blocking his path, and as soon again become flat and indistinguishable from the sand.

Reaching a vantage point, Jack saw a group of giant shadows leaping up the slope opposite. At almost the same time, he saw the bonfire. But then the flames suddenly died down, so that the interweaving feet of the people moving to and fro on the rough terrain of stones and sand around it were left illuminated and their faces, surrounded by darkness, floated disembodied in the air.

The only thing he could identify was the shrill voice of Keeko, laughing.

At that moment, Jack stumbled against a mass of something blacker than the darkness and, involuntarily putting a hand on it to steady himself, apologized to it. His hand had touched something sweaty yet smooth and unnaturally cold to the touch: the flesh of a shoulder that was like well-kneaded black clay.

"No problem," said Harry the black, giving a preliminary slap to the conga drum held between his knees, which sent a series of sluggish beats echoing around the surrounding hills.

The crowd that hung out in the modern jazz cafe had had the idea of giving summer a send-off by holding a party, a rather offbeat party, somewhere by the sea. There on the sand they would do the twist, and a whole roast pig would be served. They also

17

felt there should be some kind of primitive dance ritual, even if it was inevitably of somewhat uncertain pedigree.

In great excitement, they had split up to search for a suitable place, finally settling on this uninhabited valley. The members of the group who'd gone out to a suburb of Tokyo to buy the pig had been short of funds, and had come back shouldering half a pig instead.

Who would have thought that here, not far from that tawdry beach where the boring bourgeoisie jostled each other in the water, they would find an untouched spot like this? For the ideal site they had pictured to themselves was, whatever else, no ordinary place, but one where their own frayed jeans would take on the luster of damask.

The site: it must be chosen, made clean, sanctified. . . . They were young people for whom neon signs, tatty movie posters, exhaust fumes, and car headlights had always served as substitutes for the light of the countryside, the scent of the fields, moss, domestic animals, wild flowers; so it was natural enough now that the stretch of sandy ground they envisaged should be like a carpet of the finest workmanship, that their ultimate starry sky should resemble a piece of jewelry of the utmost artifice.

To cure the world of its stupidity, the first requirement was a process of purification through stupidity: a thorough exaltation of what the bourgeoisie saw as stupid, even if it meant aping the bourgeois creed and its single-minded, tradesman's energy. . . .

Such was the basic scheme, as it were, of the party for which thirty or forty had gathered here in the middle of the night—which to them meant business hours, their own all-important daytime. . . .

The bonfire, having suddenly died down, was smoldering, then abruptly flaring up again. This was due, Jack realized, to fat from the pig, already being roasted on a thick spit; from time to time someone was basting it with a cheap red wine. The face of the person was unidentifiable, the hands alone appearing, detached amidst the flames, as they performed their task.

Harry the black's drum was still beating, and a number of figures on the sand were doing the twist. The sand was strewn with stones, so they planted their soles carefully, their dancing for the most part a slow swaying of the knees and hips.

Over by the bank stood crates of beer and orange juice. Some empty bottles lay among the stones, gathering the faint light of night to their surfaces.

Jack's eyes should have been used to the dark by now, yet he still couldn't identify anyone in the group. The low-creeping flames of the bonfire only made it more difficult. Here and there the brief flare of lighters and matches stabbed at the bounds of vision, making it still harder to distinguish things.

Nor did the voices help; loud laughter and excited cries alike were overwhelmed by the surrounding darkness, were themselves tinged with darkness. And all the while, the night was rent by the sound of Harry's conga drum and the shrill yells that so vividly suggested the pink cavity of his mouth.

Keeko's was the one voice recognizable. Letting it guide him, Jack went and grabbed an arm that was slender and insubstantial as the wick of a lamp.

"So you got here," she said. "You alone?"

"Right."

"The gang waited for you at Inamura-ga-saki Station. But then, we knew you're always changing your mind, so we came on ahead. It's a wonder you managed to find your way here." She pursed her lips in the dark. The movement of mouth and nearby cheek, and the gleaming whites of her eyes, were visible, so Jack greeted her in the usual way by planting his own lips on hers, applying a light friction, then withdrawing them. The ef-

19

fect was like kissing the inside of a piece of bamboo bark.

"Where's everybody?"

"Hymenara and Peter are both over there. Gogi's with them. Seems he's in a state because his girl hasn't turned up. You'd better not stir him up."

Jack had got used to his own nickname. As to what "Gogi" meant, he still had no idea.

Taking him by the hand, Keeko led him through the dancers to the place beneath the bluff where the others were sitting by a big rock.

"Jack's arrived."

Hymenara responded by slowly and sleepily raising one hand. Even at this hour he was wearing dark glasses.

Deliberately, Peter lit his lighter and passed it to and fro across his own face. Blue lines were painted around the upper rim of his eyes, sweeping up at the corners to where silver dust glittered in the firelight.

"What the hell have you done to your face?"

"Peter's going to do a show later," explained Keeko, on his behalf.

Gogi, naked to the waist, was lolling sulkily against a nearby tree. Realizing it was Jack, however, he came writhing out of the darkness and, seating himself cross-legged on a patch of sand amid the undergrowth, hailed him with beery breath:

"Hi!"

Jack wasn't particularly taken with Gogi, but Gogi on his side was persistent in demonstrations of affection, and had once brought a girl with him to visit Jack in his room.

He went in for body-building, and was vain about his physique. He was almost aggressively muscular, the slightest movement of his limbs sending quick quivers of movement through chains of linked tendons. On the meaninglessness of life and the stupidity of human beings he and the rest were in theory agreed, but unlike the others he had gone to such lengths in building up a screen of muscles against the winds of despair that he had ended up fast asleep, asleep in that darkness of blind strength which is, essentially, what muscles are all about.

The thing that bothered Jack about this entity called Gogi was its non-transparent quality. Whenever it planted itself in front of him, it shut off his own view of the world, clouding with its sweaty, musky body the crystal that he always worked so hard to keep clear. Gogi's constant flaunting of his strength was intensely irritating. The insistent odor of his armpits, the hair that grew all over his body, the unnecessarily loud voice—everything made its presence as plain as filthy underwear even here in the darkness.

It was a similar disgust, oddly upsetting, that made Jack now come out with something he wouldn't normally have said:

"You know something? It was a night just like this when I tried to kill myself. Just about the same time the year before last. Today you could all have been attending my second memorial service. I mean it, really."

"If they cremated Jack," came the voice of Hymenara, tinged with a disagreeable mirth, "I guess he'd just melt, like a piece of ice. . . ."

Either way, Jack was cured by now. He'd been mistaken in thinking that if he killed himself the sordid bourgeois world would perish with him. He'd lost consciousness and been taken to a hospital, and when he came to and surveyed his surroundings, the same world had been all around him, alive and kicking as ever. So, since the world seemed irremediable, he'd resigned himself to getting better. . . .

After a while Peter got up and, leading Jack toward the bonfire, said:

21

"Do you know Gogi's girl?"

"No."

"She's a stunner, according to Gogi. Not that *that's* anything to go by. So long as she hasn't stood him up completely, she'll probably turn up sometime before morning."

"How do you know she's not here already? In this darkness you couldn't make out her lovely mug anyway, so her ladyship's idea is probably to let him discover her by the light of dawn. Much more effective."

A faint stirring of the air brought an unmistakable whiff of fat-smelling smoke, and the two of them averted their faces.

Jack set off to get some beer. Short though the way was, he stumbled over a variety of rocks, Boston bags, and recumbent forms that yielded to the touch. One couple that lay in a tightly wrapped bundle, lips joined, failed to stir even when one of Jack's rubber sandals flipped against them.

He wondered where Gogi's girl was. She might be one of that vivacious group of new faces; or again, she could be lurking behind that clump of undergrowth in the dark, or behind the smoke-wreathed stand of trees. Surely, though, if her looks were really so stunning, a faint glow would penetrate the darkness, indicating their whereabouts? Such a beautiful face ought to reveal itself by its own light, wherever it might be in that black valley or amidst the sea breezes that filled the starry sky. . . .

"Right—the ceremony's beginning! The ceremony! We'll hand out the roast pig when the dancing's over, OK? Come on, stoke up the fire!" The bellowing voice, slurred as usual by barbiturates, belonged to Hymenara. His dark glasses were thrust close to the fire, the reflection of its flames forming two miniature paintings in the lenses.

The sound of the conga drum had stopped, since Harry was

tightening its skin over the flame of a candle. For a moment, the people in the valley were silent too. Like fireflies, the glow of cigarettes swelled and shrank here and there in the shadows.

Having at last found a bottle of beer, Jack asked a stranger, a young man whose white teeth gleamed in the darkness near him, to open the bottle. He did it, expertly, with the same powerful teeth; white foam ran from his mouth down the front of his shirt, and the white teeth flashed once more in a triumphant smile.

The drum had started throbbing again, and was gradually speeding up. As Peter, in nothing but a pair of swimming trunks, began to run about the fire it blazed up, and the colored patterns and silver dust with which his body was daubed gleamed dully in its light.

Jack failed to understand Peter's excitement. Why, exactly, was he dancing? Because he was dissatisfied about something? Because he was happy? Or because it was at least better than killing himself?. . .

What exactly did Peter believe in, wondered Jack in his transparency, watching Peter's body dancing, glinting, in the light of the bonfire. Had it all been lies, then—what Peter had once told him of the misery that settled on him every night like a heavy, sodden wad of cotton? Why, when solitude howling like the sea bestrode the gaudy lights of the nocturnal city, should one proceed to *dance*?

That was the point, Jack himself was convinced, at which everything stopped. He, at least, had stopped. And then, little by little, he had become transparent. . . .

Yet after all, he reflected, dancing was a signal: an intermittent signal drawn out from somewhere deep inside human beings by some unknown agent. Peter was scattering such signals in the darkness about him now, as though scattering cards of

23

many colors. . . . Before he realized it, Jack's own foot had begun to beat time.

As Peter's body bent backward, the white of an eye ringed with eye shadow shone in the flames like a great tear in the black night. Before long, a young man in a leopardskin loincloth appeared grasping a scimitar in one hand and dangling a live white chicken, trembling, from the other. It was Gogi.

The muscles of Gogi's sweaty chest moved lustrous into the firelight. Jack saw nothing but a dark shimmer of copper flesh, darker even than the night surrounding it.

"Hey, watch him go!" cried the people around him. What could Gogi be setting out to prove? By now, his brawny arm was forcing the chicken against a rock. The chicken struggled, scattering white down that swiftly, as in a dream, was caught up in the draft of the fire and whirled high into the air. The soaring of those feathers! How well Jack knew it, that weightless flight of the emotions at the moment of the body's agony. . . .

Thus it happened without his seeing it. The callous sound came of the knife descending, and there on the stone, deaf to the cries, blind to the blood, the chicken lay twisted, its head and body parted.

Wildly plucking up the head, Peter rolled about on the sand: now, at last, Jack could appreciate his rapture. When he finally stood up again, a trickle of blood was clearly visible on the flat, boyish chest.

The head itself must have been puzzled to find things ending like this, in such a frivolous death, as part of a stunt. Its eyes no doubt, earnestly open, were full of inquiry . . . but Jack didn't look. This jesting beatification, this chance glory that had befallen the chicken crowned with its red comb, had cast a faint, scarlet reflection within his own cold, utterly uncruel heart.

And yet—he told himself—I feel nothing. Nothing at all.

Still grasping the white bird's head, Peter got to his feet and began to dance, then whirl, in a widening circle, till finally he was up against the spectators, singling out the women and thrusting the head into their faces as he rotated.

Screams ran around the ring of onlookers. Why, Jack wondered, did women's cries all sound the same? Yet even as he wondered there rose to the starry sky, then died away, a cry conspicuous for its beauty, for its clarity, for an almost tragic quality. He couldn't remember ever hearing it before. And it seemed to him that the cry must, at last, have come from that "stunning" girl of Gogi's.

Jack was a sociable fellow.

That was why—half-awake, half-asleep—he stayed on the sand or in the scrub till morning, was bitten by many mosquitoes, went swimming with the group in the daytime and, utterly exhausted, went back to his apartment in Tokyo, where he promptly fell into a deep sleep. When he awoke, his tiny room was dreadfully quiet. Why should the morning be so dark, he wondered, and looked at the clock. It was still eleven at night on the same day.

He had been sleeping with the window open, but not a breath of air came in, and his body was like a wet rag, soaked with sweat. Switching on the fan, he got his *Chants de Maldoror* from the bookshelf and lay, face down, on the bed to read.

He started to reread his favorite section, the one about the nuptials of Maldoror and the shark.

. . . What is that army of sea monsters cleaving the waves at such speed?

It was six sharks.

. . . But what, again, is that commotion of the waters, over there, on the horizon?

It was a huge, lone, female shark, the shark that was eventually to be Maldoror's bride.

The alarm clock placed by his pillow, undaunted by the humming of the fan, was marking off the time with a dull tocking. The clock was a sardonic embellishment to his daily life, for he had never once used it to wake him. His consciousness flowed on, day and night, like a murmuring brook; he was long used at night to maintaining himself transparent like crystal within it, and the alarm clock was the friend, the Sancho Panza, that turned the custom into a comedy on his behalf. The cheap sound of its mechanism was a splendid source of comfort: it made a farce of any continuity in him.

The clock, the eggs he fried for himself, the season ticket that had long ago run out—and then, the shark: yes, most definitely the shark, Jack thought forcibly. . . .

The previous evening's pointless, and more than pointless, party came back to him.

The chicken's head, the charred pig . . . and, most wretched of all, the dawn. They had all been hoping for a beautiful dawn, a splendid dawn, the kind of dawn you'd be lucky to see in a thousand years. But the reality, sad to say, had been a dawn too unsightly to bear contemplation, the very dregs of dawn.

As the first glimmerings of pale light illuminated the western side of their valley, they had seen that the trees adorning their untouched sanctuary were no more than a commonplace patch of the kind you could see anywhere, wilting in the salt breezes. Yet there was worse to come. As the light slowly slid down the western slope, it filled the gully with a bleaching-powder white that pitilessly laid it all bare—the wrecks of empty beer, juice, and Coke cans; the collapsed and smoldering bonfire; the ugly gnawings on the corncobs flung about the ground; the litter of bags of various kinds; the half-open mouths of the crowd sleeping in each other's arms by the rocks, in the scrub or on the sand; the sparse growth of moustache over some of those mouths and the sparse lipstick left on the rest; the scattered newspaper (how wretched here, though so poetic when blown about nocturnal streets!). The slaughtered remnants of a typical bourgeois outing. . . .

Some of the crowd had vanished in the course of the night, and at dawn Gogi was nowhere to be seen.

"Gogi's not here," Peter had said. "I expect he cleared out because his girl never turned up. He worries about appearances a lot more than you'd think."

A time came, a cursed time, when I grew in beauty and innocence; all admired the intelligence and virtue of this divine adolescent. Many consciences blushed to behold the features, so transparent, in which his soul sat enthroned. None approached him but with veneration, for there was apparent in his eyes the gaze of an angel.

Jack's idea of an angel might well have been fostered by this passage from *Maldoror*. Tick-tock, tick-tock: the snickering of the bedside clock seemed to discourage any answer. A dim vision of roast angel came into his head. Perhaps he was hungry.

In the sea where wrecked ships lay sunk—in some sea, surely, lay that ship wrecked with its full cargo of the world's wealth, and love, and meaning of every kind. . . . Glass scales, tilting in the distant sky. . . . The gentle panting of three dogs along the sandy shore. . . . Just before his attempted suicide, Jack had felt that he held the world like a dice in the palm of his hand, shaking it. Was there any reason why a dice shouldn't be round? A single, round dice, turning up every number in rapid succession, so that decision was suspended and the game never consummated. . . .

Jack *was* hungry. That explained it all. Standing up, he went

27

and opened the cupboard. He didn't have a refrigerator.

Nothing to eat.

The swimming man and the female shark rescued by him face each other. For several minutes, they hold each other's gaze. . . .

Quite suddenly, Jack felt he might starve if he didn't eat something. He shook the rice cracker can. Nothing but the faint sound of crumbs at the bottom. At the back of the shelf an orange lay rotting, caved in with green mold. Just then, he noticed a file of small red ants running along the edge of the cupboard. Squashing them carefully one by one, gulping down the saliva that gathered at the back of his tongue, he finally discovered, in the depths of the cupboard, half a loaf of raisin bread that he'd laid in, then forgotten all about.

Several of the ants had eaten their way into the bread between the raisins. Jack brushed them out without ceremony, then went and lay face down again on the bed, where he scrupulously examined the surface of the bread beneath the light of the lamp. He picked out two more ants.

When he sank his teeth into the bread, it tasted part bitter, part sour. He couldn't afford to let the taste bother him, so he began to gnaw into it from one end, a little at a time so as to conserve his provisions for the long night to come. The inside of the loaf was oddly soft.

They swam around in circles, never losing sight of each other, and each thinking: "I was wrong: here is another who is uglier than I."

Thus with one accord, beneath the water, they glided toward each other in mutual admiration, the female shark cleaving the water with her fins, Maldoror flailing the water with his arms. . . .

Time passed.

For some while now there had been the clatter of still-shod feet in the corridor outside and the sound of bodies colliding with the thin wooden walls, but since the other inhabitants of the apartment house often came home late Jack had paid them no attention. He got up and went, still gnawing on the raisin bread, to open the door. As he did so a man and woman came collapsing into the room like a screen falling suddenly forward. The room gave a great shudder and the bedside lamp fell over.

Closing the door behind him Jack gazed down with little surprise at his nocturnal visitors. The boy was Gogi, his aloha shirt rucked up to reveal sturdy back muscles.

"You might at least take your shoes off," said Jack. At this, the couple stretched out hands toward each other, casually took off each other's shoes and flung them in the direction of the entrance, then shook with waves of laughter. Their breath spread a reek of alcohol throughout the tiny room. Jack gazed attentively at the girl's pallid face with its closed eyes and the smile playing around the mouth. She was a stranger to him, and she was incredibly beautiful.

The face, aware of being looked at despite the closed lids, was prim even in its intoxication, and the neat, well-shaped nose, though breathing heavily, retained a porcelain stillness. The hair, which covered half her forehead, fell in attractive waves. Beneath the slight swell of her closed eyelids the eyeballs moved secretly and sensitively, the long, regular lashes held profoundly closed. The lips were exquisitely fashioned and the dimples into which they narrowed at the ends were as pristine as though carved there a moment before. Yet the face as a whole had the kind of mature dignity that only a woman of twenty-four or -five could show.

So this was the "stunning" girl, thought Jack as he went on eating the raisin bread. Gogi must have spent the whole day searching for her and brought her all the way here just to recover lost face.

29

"I don't have any quilts. There are two or three cushions if you want them. . . ." Gogi did not reply but smiled at the corners of his eyes. This, no doubt, was his evening for not saying anything.

Scraping three cushions together with his foot, Jack kicked them over behind Gogi's back, then returned to his bed, lay on his belly again, and went on eating and reading.

Sounds of protest soon came from the girl and gradually grew louder, so, putting down his book, Jack raised himself on one elbow and gazed in their direction. Gogi was already naked, the muscles moving beneath his damp, shiny skin. The girl, though down to her bra and panties by now, was still affecting delirious cries of resistance. Her body was a heap of smooth, gardenia-colored flesh.

After a while she became quiet, so Jack turned his back on them again and nibbled the raisin bread as he read.

Behind him, the expected small cries and heavy breathing failed to materialize. This eventually began to bother him. Taking another look, over his shoulder, he found that the woman was now quite naked. Locked together, the two of them were making breathy noises not unlike the grumblings of a steam train whose departure has been delayed. From Gogi's brawny back the sweat was dripping down onto the tatami.

Finally, Gogi turned his face in Jack's direction. The look of power had gone, replaced by an ambiguous, hazy smile.

"It's just no good. Lend a hand, will you, Jack?"

Nibbling the raisin bread, Jack stood up.

As he did so, he caught sight of the mark of his friend's masculinity, a half-dispirited lump of muscle. Lazily, like an indolent referee, he made his way around their heads to the other side.

"What am I supposed to do?"

"Keep tugging good and hard on her leg. That should do the trick somehow."

As though retrieving a fragment of a body run over by a train, Jack grasped one of the girl's ankles and raised it up and out. Beyond its smooth whiteness he glimpsed something briefly, as a traveler glimpses the light of a distant hut. The leg, though not particularly sweaty, slipped in his hand, so turning around he took it in his right hand. Thus he found himself standing with his back to the two of them, facing a wall that was bare save for a beer brewer's calendar. As he gnawed at the loaf in his left hand, he passed the time reading the calendar:

August 5 Sunday
6 Monday
7 Tuesday   (Dog Day)
8 Wednesday   (First Day of Autumn, lunar calendar)
9 Thursday
10 Friday
11 Saturday
12 Sunday
13 Monday
14 Tuesday
15 Wednesday   (Anniversary of End of World War II)
16 Thursday
17 Friday
18 Saturday
19 Sunday

As Gogi's and the girl's breathing started to vie with each other in what seemed to be a new lease of energy, the leg dangling from his hand moved busily, transmitting ripples of motion to him; it grew steadily weightier, with no sign of wishing to escape from its yoke. The raisin bread was bitter and sour as ever, and the more he ate the more it clung around his mouth.

After a while, Jack began to find it difficult to believe that the thing suspended from his right hand was really a woman's leg, so to make quite sure he took another look at it in the distant light of the bedside lamp. The red varnish on the toenails had peeled slightly, and the nail of the little toe was an oddly indeterminate shape, the nail itself half-buried in the flesh. A callus caused by wearing high-heeled shoes was in contact with Jack's middle finger.

Eventually, there were indications that Gogi had got up. Sure enough, a hand tapped him on the shoulder.

"That'll do," said Gogi. Jack let the leg fall to the floor.

Without further ado Gogi pulled on his trousers and, taking his aloha shirt in one hand, walked toward the door.

"So long, then," he said as he went. "Thanks. I'll leave the after-service to you."

Jack heard the door being closed. Looking down at the girl lying stretched on the floor, he put the last piece of raisin bread in his mouth and masticated dryly and at length. He touched the girl's inner thigh stealthily with his foot, but the girl was playing dead and didn't stir. He seated himself cross-legged between her parted legs. Like water from a burst main, meaninglessness came welling up from all sides with tremendous force. So he was supposed to see to the "after-service," was he? Trust Gogi to make such a comically condescending request! He bent to bring his face closer. Unnecessary obeisance: she might play dead, but her belly was rising and falling healthily, and Jack's alarm clock was marking the passage of time with a dreadfully vulgar tick-tock, tick-tock.

Arms and fins entwined the body of the loved one, embracing it

32

with passion, while throats and breasts by now were but a blue-green mass that gave off an odor of seaweed. . . .

SWORD

1

The Kokubu family crest with its design of a twin-leafed gentian gleamed gold on the black-lacquered breastplate.

In the broad band of late afternoon sun striking through the window of the fencing hall, the sweat that scattered from Kokubu Jiro's dark blue, quilted tunic glittered as it flew.

The sides of his pleated kimono skirt gave glimpses of sleek amber thigh, alive and stirring in a way that hinted at the young body dancing within the uniform and protective gear that covered him from head to foot.

Everything in his movements seemed to emanate from the essential calm suggested by the somber indigo of his dress.

One noticed him immediately on entering the hall. His body, and his alone, seemed enveloped in a kind of stillness that arose from the absolute economy of each position he assumed.

The positions were unfailingly beautiful, never doing violence to the natural postures of the body. However fierce the movement, he was always there motionless at its core; like the string of a bow after the arrow is released, he reverted at once to the original taut, yet natural and relaxed, position.

The left foot followed the right like its shadow and, as the stamp of the right foot rang increasingly loud, fell in with it to create a rhythm like the pounding of white-crested waves.

No one was surprised that he should have been selected as one of the five best fencers to represent East Japan in the East-West championship singles. The university's fencing club was proud to have him as its captain.

Mibu, a first-year student, stepped forward to have Jiro take him on for a training bout. Jiro's face, sweaty inside its metal guard, was directly before his eyes. Jiro's gaze rested on him: quiet, placid, precisely what had always been referred to in the fencing world as "the Kannon gaze."

Mibu flung himself into the warm-up session that preceded the bout itself. His bamboo sword whirled with exaggerated fury above his head.

"Face! Face! Face!" His own cry along with the explosive impact of the sword awoke a joyless, almost hysterical frenzy in his mind.

"Face! Face! Face!" The cry tore through his nostrils, brought the red blood flushing to his throat.

The warm-up ended. The two of them faced each other, swords held horizontal.

Mibu's been getting better lately, thought Jiro. Nevertheless, seen through Jiro's eyes, even the most furious moves made by the younger student seemed leisurely, as in a slow-motion film. His positions came in an unhurried, discrete sequence. As though he were a diver with his feet on the seabed who, kicking at the sand to raise himself, sends it surging slowly up around him, he scattered an invisible sand that swirled up in the water, then sluggishly settled back again.

Jiro sensed his own complete adequacy and unhurried freedom in the very sweat that seeped steadily into his eyes. The opponent's movements showed up all the more distinctly, all the more in slow time.

For all Mibu's tensely held breath, for all the busyness of his body, his face guard, gauntlets, and breastplate dangled openings as obvious as though he had hung placards there to indicate them.

They were blank windows, openings where time was suspended, yawning wide in the air. One such opening was plainly visible over Mibu's head. Another was conspicuous on the gauntlet of his straining right arm. Jiro's sword could find a way in there with the greatest of ease.

The movements of Mibu's feet were becoming less controlled. Through his face guard, white flecks were visible around his gasping mouth. The wavering of his wooden sword when their two weapons interlocked showed that his hands were trembling.

Mibu sensed that his own strength had reached its limit. Yet still he felt there was something left to come. Yes, there was something waiting: a kind of wide, empty plain filled with a white light.

"Watch it—you're getting careless!" Jiro's cries of admonition came in faint bursts from somewhere far away.

To Mibu, Jiro's presence was a lofty barrier of dark blue against which his own skills and stamina were of no avail. The relentlessness of the feeling exhausted him. Briefly, he wondered just what was waiting for him on the other side of the breathlessness and the pain in his side and the sweat. . . .

"Right! Cool off!" At last the word came from Jiro. The voice was relaxed, with no sign of tiredness.

Mibu took a rest, then, having lost the chance to take on the vice-captain, Murata, presented himself before Kagawa for a practice bout.

They saluted each other. They moved forward and crouched. They drew their swords, briefly joined the tips of the blades, stood up.

By now the training session was at its height, and the hall resounded with the thwack of bamboo swords, fierce yells, and the tamping of feet on the floor. The floor of the hall, old but resilient, throbbed beneath the tread of the club members, a good forty of them in all. Across everything, a setting May sun sent three bands of light, each the width of a window and speckled with golden dust.

Sweat splattered the floor, and it grew hot and stuffy inside the dark blue, padded uniforms. The whole atmosphere was oppressive with the surging energy the hall was struggling to contain.

Mibu was still tired, his pulse still racing, from his encounter with the club's captain. At the beginning of the bout, his own stamina had been like a country road beneath the midday sun, stretching smooth and uninterrupted as far as the eye could see. But now that the captain had done with him, the sun had suddenly set on the way, leaving him with an uneasy feeling that a little farther on the road would peter out without warning, perhaps plunge him into some waiting void.

His opponent, moreover, was Kagawa.

Kagawa was a good swordsman too, but he tended to be overbearing in his manner, and to rely on sheer strength. It was not without reason that he hadn't even been elected vice-captain: in his training sessions, in his fencing as such, there were remnants of personal emotion, of intellectual activity; he lacked the single-minded intensity of a Jiro.

"Right—warm up!" he bellowed as though impatient to start.

Mibu went in to engage him. The opening phase went on and on, but Kagawa made no move to end it.

Kagawa studied Mibu's earnest, youthful face, damp with effort inside its mask. The eyes were wide, the cheeks aflame, the whole countenance that of a young prisoner raging behind the grille of the metal guard.

This guy thinks Kokubu is the best in the world, he thought snidely. If Kagawa found himself obliged to share, to whatever

40

extent, in a respect directed primarily toward another person, his one concern was to find something false in it. . . . He felt more comfortable, if anything, when he detected hostility on the other side. Calling a halt at last to the warm-up session, he took satisfaction in the other's labored breathing.

Now the attack practice. "Forearm! Face!" In rapid succession Mibu tried out his techniques, aiming at first one point then another on the other's body, drawing back as necessary each time and closing in again without respite.

But Kagawa obstinately refused to let himself be touched: he felt no inclination to ease up in order to encourage his opponent.

Imbued with a desperate strength, the tip of Mibu's sword rose into the air. Once more it was turned aside. Kagawa moved around him, the late afternoon sun gleaming red on the metal of his face guard. The mask was here one moment, there the next, now dim against the daylight sun, now raw red in its light. Mibu brought his sword down where it should have been, only to find it gone.

Mibu's cries grew fainter and hoarser as he gradually tired from swinging vainly at his opponent.

Parried, halted in midair, his sword, deprived of what it had been so fiercely seeking, found itself cleaving to a point of emptiness. To recover in a moment the balance thus upset and extricate the sword from the nothingness in which it was lodged required exceptional strength.

Checking his body as it tottered forward, Mibu pulled himself upright, looking like a dark blue heron as he did so.

"Right—three-set match!" cried Kagawa, observing his fatigue.

At that moment, as he called to his opponent, there was a chink in Kagawa's mental armor: the merest instant of self-indulgent fantasy, of hedonistic interest in the feeble prey before his eyes, of almost prurient pleasure in his own strength. . . .

It was the greedy, animal kind of pleasure that cannot be experienced fully when alone nor savored at leisure face to face with another. A pleasure unrelated either to memory or hope, a dangerous pleasure of the present moment, akin to that of riding a bicycle no-hands. . . .

A shadow flashed past Kagawa's eyes.

By the time he realized it, he was done for.

"Face!" A resounding stamp of a foot, and Mibu's bamboo sword had crashed down in a desperate last blow to his mask.

"It's yours. Second set," said Kagawa languidly.

Kokubu Jiro left the area, reserved for senior fencers, where he'd been standing and took his place before the club's coach, Kinouchi, in order to be put through his paces. When Kinouchi wasn't present, everyone in the club referred to him as Tenouchi, or "the Grip," since he never lost an opportunity to insist that a "correct grip was everything."

At fifty, this veteran was the most revered among former members of the fencing club. He'd once run a company of his own, but had left it in the charge of its managing director, his younger brother, and come back to his old college to devote himself to the club.

As Jiro came forward, Kinouchi could sense the cool determination that his bearing proclaimed. Jiro advanced toward him in a straight line, the blue pleated skirt of his uniform billowing slightly in time with the regular rise and fall of his feet, which barely left the ground.

Kinouchi felt an affection for the youthfulness thus challenging him. Youth came to the attack courteously yet brutally, while age awaited it, a smile on its lips, without stirring and with confidence. Courtesy without violence was displeasing in a young man, less acceptable even than violence without courtesy.

Youth would come lunging at him—lunging only, inevitably, to submit. Youth and he shared the same training clothes, the same protective armor, the same sweat. . . . For Kinouchi, the fencing hall afforded an interval of pure beauty, of time that had stopped forever. Within that time, the black breastplate gleamed, the purple cords of the face guard flew, the sweat scattered—exactly as he had experienced it thirty years earlier, here in his old school.

In that shared context, age concealing its gray hairs in a face guard, and youth concealing its ruddy cheeks in similar armor, confronted each other as adversaries, unequivocally, with the simplicity of an allegory. It was as though life and its welter of extraneous matter had been reduced to the clean simplicity of a chessboard. Filter everything else away and this, surely, was all that was left: this once-and-for-all confrontation, sword tip to sword tip, one day in a strong sunset light, between age and youth.

The warm-up over, Jiro stood with his sword directed toward the older man's eyes, waiting for him to offer an opening.

Kinouchi's style of swordsmanship was unemphatic; the tip of his weapon always maintained a distance, feeling its way softly, light as a feather: it was his most dangerous aspect. Surveying him, Jiro saw only a seamless perfection. Yet it was not like gazing at, say, a closed door of steel; rather, it suggested a Japanese-style room flung open to a summer's day, deserted, nothing there but the tatami in their simple purity. It was that kind of perfection.

Kinouchi seemed to have no point of support, but to float, almost, in the air.

Jiro gave a high-pitched yell. Slowly, he edged around to the right.

Kinouchi was like a transparent cone that presented the same aspect from whatever angle it was viewed. No way in here: he moved further to the right. Then, swiftly, back to the left: no opening here, either. Jiro felt humiliated by his own obviousness.

On the far side of this frustration Kinouchi lounged like a great indigo cat taking a daytime nap.

Jiro gave up any idea of finding a weak point. It must be his own impatience, he felt, that prevented him from getting at him. The other man's flawlessness was surely a false front, a sleight of hand; in this world, nothing could really be so perfect.

A thin casing of ice seemed gradually to be enveloping his person, threatening to encase his shoulders and elbows firmly till finally he was trapped in it. The more he put things off, the worse it got. He must burst out with all the strength of his body, smash the ice.

Up flew the purple of Jiro's helmet strings in fine style. Forth went his strength. He leaped, gave a cry, with the suddenness of a pigeon starting up from the cage that confined it.

In a flash, cutting through all the splendid speed, something diverted Jiro's weapon upward, and down on his head like a brand of burning steel fell the heavy blow of Kinouchi's sword.

2

Jiro had been made captain of the club in spring that year, appointed by his seniors in a move that he had always felt would come in the natural course of events.

He had come to feel his own prowess as something self-evident. At some point or other, it had become a kind of transparent garment sheathing his person, one of whose very existence he could be oblivious.

"I'll do the best I can," he had said in his speech on being made captain. "Physically and spiritually, I'll put everything I've got into it. If you follow me, you won't go wrong, I assure you. Those who feel they can follow me, please do so. Those who can't—do as you like."

As he spoke—to forty club members, in the presence of his predecessors—Jiro had come to a decision.

He had long since felt that on this occasion he would speak to this effect, and he had done so. It was the fulfillment of a presentiment. For years the words had remained furled within his mind, and at the right moment they had spread their wings and taken flight.

With them, he had finally put aside the ordinary, boyish qualities still lurking inside him. Mental softness and impressionability—rebelling, scorning, lapsing occasionally into self-disgust—were to be discarded entirely. A sense of shame was to be retained, but bashful hesitation was to go.

Any feelings of "I want to" must be done away with, to be replaced, as a basic principle, by "I should."

Yes—that was what he would do. He would focus the whole of his daily life on fencing. The sword was a sharp-pointed crystal of concentrated, unsullied power, the natural form taken by the spirit and the flesh when they were honed into a single shaft of pure light. . . . The rest was mere trivia.

To be strong and true had been the most important task he had set himself since early childhood.

Once, as a boy, he had tried to outstare the sun. But before he could tell whether he had really looked at it or not, changes had occurred: the blazing red ball that had been there at first began to whirl, then suddenly dimmed, till it became a cold, bluish-black, flattened disk of iron. He felt he had seen the very essence of the sun. . . .

For a while, wherever he looked he saw the sun's pale afterimage: in the undergrowth; in the shade beneath the trees; even, when he gazed up, in every part of the sky.

The truth was something too dazzling to be looked at directly. And yet, once it had come into one's field of vision, one saw patches of light in all kinds of places: the afterimages of virtue.

Thus he would gird himself in strength and clothe himself in righteousness. For all he knew, he was the only person in the world who looked at things in that way; it was a wonderfully original outlook.

Cheating at school, minor infringements of various regulations, laxity in matters of loans to and from one's friends—it was strange how such things were considered a mark of youth. As he saw it, there was only one choice—to be strong and upright, or to commit suicide. When a fellow from his own class killed himself, Jiro had approved of the act in itself, yet had felt it a pity that it wasn't the strong man's suicide he had always envisaged, but that of someone frail in both mind and body.

The classmate, they said, had been found dead of an overdose of sleeping pills, in bed, his face the color of the sheets. In bed with him lay the peel of some loquats he'd eaten, together with five or six large, glossy seeds. Perhaps, as the pills began to take effect, he had tried to assuage the dread of looming unconsciousness by stuffing himself with fruit.

The loquat peel and seeds—the bodily appetite in the human being about to die—these bothered Jiro, who tried to distance himself from them as far as possible. He had already taken up fencing at the time.

The sword cleft the air of its own volition. When things went well at least, it really seemed as though this were so. Even without his taking aim, it winged home on that merest hairsbreadth of inattention shown by the adversary, delivering its blow with accuracy.

It was as though—how should he put it?—it was as though a vacuum of energy occurred there momentarily, so that the free-flowing stream of one's own energy was drawn, inevitably, toward it. It was necessary that this personal strength should be utterly free and utterly uncommitted, otherwise it got caught up in things and failed to be drawn on so effortlessly.

He'd had the experience any number of times. To achieve it, the only way was unremitting practice, unremitting physical toil.

If in the bus on the way to college he saw an elderly woman standing, or a woman with a child, he would get up smartly and give her his seat. Sometimes these women would thank him repeatedly as they sat down, and again when he got off. But his own boy-scout behavior gave Jiro no particular sense of pleasure; in fact he was glad, on reflection, to discover that he got no gratification from it at all.

It was enough that his perception of what was right should mark out peripheries within which everything was swept and tidy. Innocent of any interest in politics or the workings of society, he retrieved from them just such snippets of knowledge as were necessary for his own purposes. The "trivial" chatter of his fellows he listened to in smiling taciturnity. Books he read not at all.

He had been born, he felt, into a peculiar age, one in which to devote oneself to one thing, to be able to resist the lure of the trivial, to have simple, uncomplicated aims—such perfectly ordinary qualities—had become something rare and isolating for the individual.

One afternoon in late spring Jiro, finding that a lecture on administrative law had been canceled, followed an impulse and went alone to the fencing hall. There was some time yet before practice began, and the hall was empty, the only reminder of humanity a faint, insistent smell of sweat.

Alone, he changed into his training gear and advanced to the center of the spotlessly gleaming floor; it was as though he were walking across the dark surface of some holy lake. He stamped on the floor: it responded. Taking out his bamboo sword, he did three hundred practice strokes at an imaginary opponent, counting each stroke aloud.

It was a gloriously beautiful day. Pressing his face into a cotton towel that someone had left hanging to dry on a pole, he wiped off the worst of the sweat.

Then, still in training uniform with his sword at his side, he went around the back of the hall and climbed the slope behind it, which lay at the northern extremity of the university campus. There was no one in sight in the space between the scattered trees, and putting his sword down on the grass he lay back and stretched out his legs, in their pleated skirt, before him. He hadn't gone out of his way to be alone, yet this spell of solitude after exercise, as the remaining sweat receded with the speed of an ebb tide, gave him a sense of vitality more satisfying than at any other time. Below the sharp drop on the other side of the slope stretched a factory district whose drifting smoke distorted the prospect of modern office buildings that lay still farther beyond it.

It wasn't that he was waiting for anything. But as he looked at

48

the clear sky and the lazy wisps of cloud and heard fitfully, from amidst the low roar of the industrial area, the bright pinpoints of cars' horns, he sensed, somehow, the approach of some high adventure. What it would be he couldn't tell, yet the suggestion was that he was about to play a part, whether he willed it or not, in some tale of heroism. A swordsman in the old days would have said that he had scented blood.

The crack of a gun grazed his ear.

Immediately, there was a sound as of splashing water in the branches above his head, the foliage swayed, and down beside him fell something resembling a plump white handbag. Looking more closely, he found it was a pigeon.

One bedraggled wing dripping blood where it had been shot, it lay struggling on the grass. Gently, Jiro lifted it in his arms and inspected its trembling leg; a metal ring enclosing it told him that it belonged to the university carrier-pigeon club. Silent, the feathers of its breast heaving, the pigeon was dipping its small bare head again and again; Jiro could feel it trembling incessantly in his hand.

He stood up, with the idea of taking it back to the university. The sunlight shone on him through the trees as he stood there, sword at his side, his dark blue sleeve sheltering the bird's frail beauty.

Just then, there was a rustle of undergrowth and a group of five or six youths appeared. Such intruders often found their way into the campus via a gap in the barbed wire at the foot of the hill at the back.

All of them wore jeans, and one had an air rifle at the ready. Trampling the bamboo grass as they came up the slope, they formed a group in front of Jiro and looked at him as though peering at something in the dark.

"It's my bird—hand it over," said the youth with the rifle.

"This pigeon belongs to the university," said Jiro. "Was it you who shot it?"

"That's right. So it's mine now. Give it back." He jerked his chin, affecting a gruff voice that came out half-impatient, half-wheedling.

"What d'you mean, give it back? *I'm* the one to say that."

"Why, you—" The boy pointed his rifle at Jiro's chest. "Come on, let's have it! Don't get any fancy ideas just because you're a student."

"Shoot him! Shoot him! Go on!" muttered the other youngsters halfheartedly, huddling together.

Though their manner suggested bad temper, there was almost no sense of hostility or hatred. The only thing that clearly emanated from the group, who differed little in age from Jiro himself, was a primitive odor of immaturity. A hidden rage, the rage of an animal scenting its own kind, darkened Jiro's vision. But the wooden sword stayed passive in his grasp.

"Well—if that's what you want . . ." The boy pointed the muzzle at Jiro's chest and put a finger on the trigger.

At that moment, the sword flicked out from Jiro's hand, traversed a surprising distance, and dealt a sharp blow to the youth's wrist. The rifle fell to the grass, and as the boy bent down to retrieve it Jiro seized the opportunity to move forward silently and easily to place a foot on the barrel.

The youth leaped back. Following his cue, the rest of them turned to flee, blundering into each other in the process. Jiro calmly pressed forward, his movements relaxed, as though over a smooth, obstacle-free course.

Cursing him, they ran down the slope through the undergrowth and fled in different directions. Jiro picked up the air gun and flung it after them. One of them grabbed it up, yelling as he did so:

"You fool—getting scared when it wasn't even loaded!"

Soon they could be seen ducking though the gap in the barbed wire and disappearing up a deserted alley in the factory district.

Jiro became aware that the pigeon he held firmly clasped under his left arm was drooping its head listlessly. Alarmed, he relaxed the pressure. With unexpected vigor, the bird sprang up, shoving off from his sleeve with its claws and taking wing in a confused flutter. As it did so, blood sprayed from its wing and splashed onto Jiro's cheek.

But it had only gone about as high as his forehead when it seemed to falter. As Jiro looked up in surprise it loomed for a moment absurdly large in his field of vision, then halted in the air as though crumpled suddenly by some insane power. It gleamed in the sunlight filtering through the trees, refulgent like oil with the sheen of feathers and blood. . . .

The next moment, it flopped down again onto Jiro's left arm. The anger of a while ago, temporarily repressed, flashed through his mind again; obliged to assume a serene form, it had achieved its serene victory, but now in reverse it engulfed him in dark waves. Tucking the sword under his left arm, he brought his right hand near the pigeon's throat.

The sound of wheels came from the path through the college grounds.

Aroused from his murderous intent, Jiro turned to look. The school's elderly handyman was coming along with his trash cart.

A suspicion that his purpose had been perceived brought a flush to Jiro's cheeks. The old man was taking his cart to the garbage dump on the hillside.

To help keep his self-respect, Jiro deliberately marched toward him.

"I was watching," declared the old man, a slight figure in

workman's overalls. "Nice bit of work! Good for you. Really, young people nowadays scare me—you never know what
they're going to do. I was watching from behind there. I'd heard
the shooting. . . . Here—you've got blood on your cheek. Let me
wipe it off."

Jiro hadn't brought a hand towel with him, and the old man's
pockets failed to yield a handkerchief. To Jiro's consternation,
he began to rummage in the trash cart, which was crammed
with a multicolored, unsavory mess of stained leaflets and bits of
old newspaper.

"It's OK," said Jiro, about to wipe it with his sleeve.

"No, wait—" Checking him peremptorily, the old handyman
took out of his cart a single, withered white lily. "This is one
of those expensive hothouse flowers—it was in a vase in the
president's room. You couldn't find anything cleaner. Come on,
let me wipe it for you."

He arranged several yellowing petals in a disproportionately
large hand, then, applying them to Jiro's cheek, wiped off the
blood with them. Jiro could smell the lily's faint, lingering scent.

"There—look how clean it's come off!"

The old man showed him the petals. The white parts, which
still retained a dull luster, had soaked up the blood, making a pattern like veins clearly visible in a fair, sensitive complexion.

"Thank you." Jiro inclined his head, the pigeon still drooping
quietly in his arms.

The garbage cart went off slowly up the path, while Jiro made
his way toward the lofts of the carrier pigeon club.

Thus all unconsciously he had come unscathed through the
several snares of poetry—the bloodied pigeon, and the sun shining among the trees; the blood that had splashed the victor's
cheek; the deep blue of the training clothes, and the faded white

lily—through all the snares that these things had conspired to set in his path.

3

Kinouchi was happy at any time to have the youngsters from his old club visit him at home. His wife, too, treated them as part of the family. Both of the Kinouchis' children, in fact, were daughters, and both had already married and left home.

Thus when Kagawa dropped in unexpectedly one evening, Kinouchi, who treated all members with complete impartiality, made him welcome.

Kinouchi was on the plump side, with a fair complexion and broad features; nothing in his mild appearance suggested the underlying strength that was actually there.

"The matter of the part-time job is all settled," he said, pouring beer into the other's glass. The fencing club was due to work at a well-known department store during the vacation, helping to wrap goods for the summer sales. "The high-ups are all well disposed to us, so it should be a good atmosphere to work in."

"It's rather dull work, though," said Kagawa.

"Sure it is," said Kinouchi mildly, refusing to be put off. "And the duller the better. The kind of part-time work that uses the brain in the wrong way isn't any good—it interferes both with your studies and your training."

"I expect Kokubu will be raring to go as usual."

"He's always raring to go. It's his chief virtue."

"The model leader as ever."

"And what's wrong with that?"

There was a short silence.

Kagawa found it difficult to tell Kinouchi of the psychological motive that had brought him there that evening. The matter was too trivial for another person to understand easily.

It was something that had happened while they were all having a bath after training the previous evening. The first-year student assigned to wait on the seniors' needs had been about to wash Jiro's back for him, a matter that normally would have required no special thought. But Jiro, glancing in Kagawa's direction, had apparently noticed that there was no one to wash his back. The younger student, a conscientious first-year fellow, probably intended to do him after finishing with the captain.

The bathhouse was old and dark, and Jiro's back, in the enveloping steam, had been a board of wet, muscular flesh. It occurred to Kagawa with dismay that he might be going to slip the junior word to give Kagawa precedence. But he hadn't done so. Without a second glance in his direction, he turned away and let the junior start lathering his broad back vigorously all over.

The slight arrogance of it—half a shock, half hoped-for—was, either way, intolerable. A simple, unconscious arrogance would at least have had the charm of naiveté. But this was a consciously chosen arrogance. Quite clearly, Jiro had noticed Kagawa but, afraid of hurting his pride by too obviously yielding him precedence, had chosen instead to "appear" arrogant; the fellow knew that in such cases he was *supposed* to be so, however people might react.

Kagawa felt an immense irritation at seeing what should have been a simple, unclouded decision leave Jiro prey in this way to a moment's clever calculation.

He hadn't always been like that, he thought, with stirring anger. But now he'd grown wary even of him, Kagawa. He'd even started to detect "misunderstanding" in Kagawa's perfectly natural responses, convincing himself that it was his fate to

54

have the people about him get him wrong. But that kind of pride just wouldn't do: friends didn't "misunderstand" each other!

Kagawa held the fourth rank in fencing, the same as Jiro, but there was a subtle difference. According to the club's own grading, which was determined by the coach and other instructors, Kagawa had been third rank until early that year, when he had reached the next rung up as a result of having himself assessed by the Fencing Association. The university's grading system was stricter than the association's. Jiro, who was fourth rank under the college system, could easily, with his ability, have got fifth rank in the association. But he'd made no move to have his skill assessed. And that was what was really weighing on Kagawa's mind.

Yet though Kagawa was capable of looking at things in this convoluted way, he still believed in friendship.

"The summer camp has me really worried," he said, "if he's going to keep up that kind of pressure."

"I imagine he's dead set on winning the national championships."

"He never seems to let up at all, does he?"

"He's young—it can't be helped."

"I'm the same age as him."

"But you're more—I'd say—grown up."

Kinouchi would listen to any amount of complaints, and never pass judgment on them.

He felt he understood the immediate reason why Kagawa reacted as he did. Almost certainly, it was because during the campus training session in May he'd been caught smoking and drinking, and had been subjected to disciplinary action.

Jiro never overlooked an infringement of the rules, even by

someone in the same year as himself. But Kinouchi knew exactly what went on in Jiro's mind when he administered punishment to a classmate.

There was a notice on the wall of the locker room: "Absence without permission, smoking, drinking, and other violations of club rules will be punished by forty minutes' *seiza*."

This was as far as such disciplinary measures usually went nowadays; to sit on your heels on a hard wooden floor for forty minutes might be tough, but it was nothing compared with the punishments of the past. Even so, it was enough to make some freshmen break out in a clammy sweat, or even faint, after thirty minutes or so.

Kinouchi could hardly avoid referring to the subject.

"It's that business of smoking, isn't it—when you got caught?"

"Don't bring that up again, please," said Kagawa, scratching his head in embarrassment.

"I'm just curious about Kokubu's attitude since then. Has he behaved normally toward you?"

"Oh yes, of course. No different from before."

"Good. But after he'd made you do the regulation forty minutes in front of all those juniors, did he say anything to you to make up for it?"

"No."

"I mean, when you and he were alone did he say, for example, 'sorry about that—it had to be done for the sake of discipline, but don't take it to heart'?"

"No, nothing like that."

"You mean, he didn't say *anything*, eh?"

"No . . . but I can understand. He's that kind of guy. . . ."

"Even so, I wonder if he shouldn't have said it."

"No—I guess he didn't think so. He just kept quiet . . . in fact, he was smiling."

"*Smiling*?"

It had been an attractive smile. Jiro's expression when he was putting up with something "trivial," something tiresome and pointless, was always the same: the same silent smile.

Kagawa was jealous of its obvious charm; it seemed to sum up the image of a clean-living young man, and was more than he could ever hope to imitate.

Jiro's was a rather small mouth, with well-shaped lips. When he smiled, revealing even white teeth, it was like a sudden burst of purity.

The silence in which he sought to settle everything with that smile, to make others appreciate the awkwardness of his own position, was what irked Kagawa. Jiro rejected any thought of saying something comforting, spurned all "diplomatic" behavior, shutting himself up in the crystal fortress of his own purity and abruptly removing himself from the reality of others' suffering. Jiro himself knew that though a smile like that, coming as it did after he had personally imposed forty minutes of *seiza* on his contemporary, might well be seen as a sneer, in fact it contained no hint of mockery. But Kagawa saw this as a kind of arrogance.

Faced with actual pain in another person—physical pain, that is, not mental—Jiro, far from smiling, would be genuinely concerned. If a younger student so much as got a tiny thorn in his toe, he would painstakingly get it out for him and paint the place with mercurochrome. If the hurt was physical, he would take care of it—like a cavalryman with his horse.

"I see . . . so he didn't say anything." Kinouchi thought for a moment. "It's a tricky business, but that kind of thing's not good enough in someone who's leader of the club. I'll have a word with him next time I see him."

"No—please don't say anything."

"I won't mention your name."

"That's not what I mean. If you give him a warning, he'll brood on it. It'll probably make him all the more sure that the people around him aren't worthy of him, and puff him up even more. With him, the best thing is to leave him be as far as possible."

"You're contradicting yourself, surely. I don't see why, with your help, he shouldn't think things over and make an effort to get back to what he used to be."

Each word of Kinouchi's contrived skillfully to coddle Kagawa's self-esteem. Kagawa, who was sensitive enough to notice this at once, wished he'd never come that evening.

As coach of the fencing club, Kinouchi's ability, experience, and personality were beyond reproach. At fifty, he blended the experienced and the childlike in just the right proportions.

Beneath his loyalty to the college, his nostalgia, his indifference to worldly reputation, festered longstanding memories of an inability to adjust to, of discontent with, the everyday world. He couldn't understand why society in general wasn't uncomplicated and beautiful, like the world of sport, why its conflicts weren't resolvable through contests whose outcome was evident to anyone. Over the years, he had elevated this resentment, common to most sportsmen, into a kind of poetry.

Why?... Each repetition of the profitless inquiry enhanced still further the beauty of sport and youth. Every comparison with the mire of society only made the hallowed ground of sport seem more attractive. . . .

It occurred to Kagawa with a sense of despair that the more he gave vent to feelings that he himself found distasteful, the more appealing he seemed in Kinouchi's eyes. Kinouchi, having experienced ordinary society, was sentimentally convinced that personal relations within the sports clubs, however much friction they might involve, were at least more acceptable than they were outside.

There was Kagawa's youth, too. The visions inspired in Kinouchi by youth—plus what was, at heart, an infinite tolerance toward it, however tough he might be as a trainer—were something that even now, as Kagawa talked to him, he could sense rising up like a fog between them.

"You'll think I'm on my hobbyhorse again," Kinouchi was saying from the depths of his armchair, making a gesture with his hands as though wringing out a cloth. "But when all's said and done, everything in fencing depends on your grip. That's the one thing I've learned from thirty-five years of it. The important thing for a human being is to learn and master one thing in his life—one thing, however small. That's enough.

"It all depends on your grip whether you make that little bit of shaped bamboo come to life or let it stay dead. It's fascinating. And in a way, as I see it, getting the knack of dealing with the world is just the same.

"People always say that you should grip with your right hand as though you were carrying an open umbrella, and with your left as though you were holding an egg. But how long do you think you can keep an umbrella up or hold an egg in your hand? Just try it—I'll bet that in thirty minutes or so at the most you'll want to throw the umbrella down and crush the egg in your fist. . . ."

Kagawa had heard it all any number of times before. It was a familiar theme; Kinouchi embarked on it whenever he drank, going through the motions of grasping an invisible sword with the rough, clumsy hands that went so oddly with his pale, placid face. His expression at such times would be impassioned, his

59

eyes following with affection the well-tempered edge of an invisible blade as he raised and lowered it.

Once the talk turned to fencing, there was no question any longer of failure of communication, whether verbal or emotional, between Kinouchi and Kagawa. The words flew to and fro, and they could talk to themselves without being alone, since every word corresponded to a remembered excitement in matches and training sessions.

Occasionally, Kinouchi threw in something calculated to amuse the younger man:

"Hey—do you know the best way to flay the skin off a face?"

"No."

"You should make a note of it as one of the necessary accomplishments of a swordsman. You'll find it in the tenth book of *Hagakure*.

"First, you make cuts at the sides, the top, and the bottom, then you piss on it, then you put on straw sandals and trample on it, and you can slip the skin off without any trouble. Apparently Gyojaku learned the traditional technique on a trip to the Kanto area."

"Wow! I must try it next time I get a chance."

"It might not work properly with someone who was too thick-skinned.... Look—," he went on, abruptly changing the subject, "to go back to what we were talking about—have you ever heard about Kokubu's family background?"

"No, he never lets any of his friends anywhere near his home. That's another thing I find difficult to understand about him."

"I'm not surprised. The father's a doctor with plenty of money, runs a respectable clinic for stomach disorders, but while Kokubu was in middle school he lost his head over some woman, and it messed up the home. The father takes no interest whatever in the children's education, and the mother gets hysterical and consoles herself with drink—goes out at ten at night to play mah-jongg at a friend's and doesn't come home till the morning. . . . It's no wonder he doesn't like talking about his family."

"I'd no idea things were so bad." Kagawa spoke in surprise, but immediately reflected that there was no call to waste any sympathy on Kokubu: Kokubu was an adult who was making a life for himself in his own way.

"Anyway, perhaps you should bear it in mind," said Kinouchi. "But don't go telling anybody. I've known the family to some extent for a long time—that's how I happen to know how things stand."

4

Mibu shaved every morning before going to school, hoping to make his beard grow more thickly, but the rest of the family said it was a waste of razor blades. Why then, he retorted, didn't they buy him an electric razor? And he went for a week without shaving, just to show them, but his beard let him down. All that appeared were a few patches of hair on his smooth, pale amber chin, which in no sense could be described as "unshaven."

In the eyes of the other members of his family, Mibu was childish for his years. His boyhood had slipped into late adolescence with none of the usual storms and tantrums.

Having an enormous respect for Jiro, he was forever talking about him at home.

"There you go again!" mother and sisters would say teasingly. "Don't you have *any* other topics of conversation?"

Frustrated, he would buttonhole his cousins when they came visiting and talk to them instead. But they soon got tired of the subject and began to avoid him.

Most young men of Mibu's age, even if they secretly revere someone, can't bring themselves to express it in words. Normally, the naive desire to appear self-sufficient makes them shy about such emotions. Mibu's family thought it a sign of childishness that he was so forthcoming on the matter.

He himself had different ideas on the subject. Jiro's serenity, his moral and physical strength, had communicated themselves to him, too, in turn, ridding him of the diffident pride of the very young. . . .

Mibu still had another year to go before qualifying to vote. The idea that he would get the vote, become an adult, and eventually settle into happy domesticity filled him with despair.

He too had on one occasion been punished by having to sit in the formal position, on his heels, for forty minutes. A club member in his first year had said something disparaging about Jiro. Mibu could never let any such criticism go uncorrected. He made the first move, a scuffle developed, and the other bled slightly from the nose. The vice-captain got wind of the fight and Jiro handed down a verdict of shared blame.

Jiro inquired into the reason for the quarrel, but Mibu, who had resolved not to tell, remained silent throughout, gazing fiercely into Jiro's eyes.

Seated on his heels on the bare board floor, his feet numb, his shins hurting and, as time went by, even his thighs beginning to quiver with the strain, Mibu had felt a sense of satisfaction at his own manliness.

Later, when the episode was over, someone had apparently informed Jiro of the cause of the quarrel. Jiro himself said nothing about it, but in the look he gave him Mibu confidently detected a silent understanding. He was grateful, moreover, that Jiro treated him not a whit differently because of it.

"Whatever is it that's so special about this captain of yours?" his mother would sometimes ask.

"Kokubu is genuine and straightforward, and tremendously tough, but he's not a bit smug about it. It's enough to make you despair—the idea that there are people like him."

"Why not hurry up and get like that yourself, then?"

"I couldn't hope to equal him."

"Precious little confidence you've got!" his mother declared with a disgusted look. "What parent would be pleased to hear their son say that kind of thing about himself?"

Whatever Mibu did turned out as an imitation of Jiro. But however much he aped his way of walking and talking he could never, he was convinced, acquire a smile as attractive, as significant-looking as his.

In Mibu's nineteen-year-old eyes, the world of adults was hopelessly repulsive, and the idea that sooner or later Jiro too would be sullied by it horrified him. If youth and genuineness and strength were something that climbed to a peak, as in Jiro, only to go tumbling down on the other side, then the world was an unspeakably depressing place. . . .

So often did Mibu rail at the depravity of his own age group that his parents began to fret about possible ideological leanings; but he was utterly innocent of any interest in politics.

He tried listing to himself the failings of modern youth, to see if any one of them applied in Jiro's case. Excessive interest in personal appearance, the search for easy sexual gratification, rebellious behavior, and loss of any aim in life, turning eventually to domesticity, a preoccupation with lawn-mowing, and hankerings after a pension—no, none of those things applied to Jiro. Outside the fencing hall, Jiro was just one more inconspicuous student, sober in appearance, who neither indulged in smutty conversation nor hung around the girls, who foreswore immature rebellion and concentrated all his aims in life on fencing, and on fencing alone. As things were at present, Jiro had no future beyond the national fencing finals.

Nothing about him, in fact, suggested any thoughts of future happiness. Although he hadn't exactly expressed it in words, his underlying creed—Mibu told himself with confident excitement—was that happiness wasn't a proper concern for a man. That, surely, was the source of his peculiar radiance....

One day, three first-year members of the club, Mibu among them, were emerging from the college gates when they met Jiro, who was just on his way home. They greeted him, and he took them to have coffee in a nearby tea shop. They were stiff with shyness, but Mibu finally managed to get a conversation going.

"H. University's still a tough opponent, isn't it? The brother of a friend of my sister is there, so I got her to take me along the other day to have a look at them training."

"How was it?"

Mibu told him briefly about the practice session.

"For one thing, their club's got plenty of money," said Jiro. "Their budget's ¥600,000 a year, and they employ a full-time coach. I hear they get a lot of contributions from graduates, too. But we're not going to be beaten by money. It's training that counts in the end. Training and nothing else!"

Just then, a burst of snickering came from three students of the same university installed in a booth close to the toilet, and they saw a customer, a young woman, rush past between the tables with her head bent to hide her face.

"They're at it again, the bastards," said one of the first-year club members.

"What are they doing?"

"Whenever they come here, they hole up in that booth there.

And they wait for a girl to go into the toilet. Look—you'll see."

All unsuspecting, another girl went into the toilet. Mibu and the rest waited, watching. Before long the girl opened the door and came out again, whereupon the students shoved their faces over the backs of their seats and set up a chorus:

"How was it? Was there a lot?"

"Feel better now, dear?"

The girl turned red and hurried past, looking close to tears.

The petty nastiness of their game was enough to send Mibu into an immediate rage. They were a disgrace to the university.

He kept his eyes on Jiro, in the expectation that anger would fetch him out of his seat; if Jiro got up, Mibu and the rest would gladly follow.

But he was silent, seemingly deep in thought. Mibu considered the possible decisions he would come to. Would he get up, grab the culprits by the scruff of the neck, march them outside, and knock them to the ground? No—Jiro wasn't likely to go in for such violent heroics. Or would he perhaps go to the toilet himself, and when he emerged call out to them sarcastically, "Oh yes, gallons of it. It was great!" No—this sort of stunt wasn't in character either.

Jiro's expression as he sat thinking produced a pleasant kind of thrill in Mibu. Almost certainly, he was dwelling on the nature of evil and iniquity. Like a small tag of old padding projecting from a torn quilt, the small visible evil they'd just witnessed would, if you tugged at it, give way to a huge gray mass of evil. Jiro's clear gaze, he felt sure, was gauging its exact extent.

All of a sudden, Jiro said,

"OK, let's change places."

Mibu felt let down: was he just going to run away from it?

There were vacant tables here and there in the tea shop, including one between themselves and the booth in question. But when Jiro got up, with Mibu and the rest following close behind, he marched straight up to the three other students.

"Hi!" he said, nodding with his usual charming smile. The trio, not recognizing him, looked at each other doubtfully.

"My name's Kokubu, I'm in the fencing club. The way you behaved is a disgrace to the college. So, come on—let's have those seats."

"Come off it—there are plenty of other seats, aren't there?"

"Right, then, you can go to a place that's empty."

"What the . . ." One of them clicked his tongue impatiently and turned aside.

"Come on, move out!" As Jiro spoke, one of the three edged out of his seat, grumbling to himself as he went. There was no further resistance; clumsily, with hunched shoulders, they got up and made to shift to the next booth. But Jiro stood in their way.

"No—you go over *there*."

They shared a comical moment of bewilderment. But Jiro, with perfectly natural movements, shepherded them straight ahead while Mibu and the rest followed in tense anticipation.

"There!" Jiro pointed to the entrance to the toilet. One of them recoiled so sharply that he stumbled.

"There—in there!" he said, advancing slowly and inexorably.

One by one, they were crammed into the toilet, which was no more than about six feet square. As the door shut on them, they looked like passengers in a tiny elevator.

Jiro sat down at the table where they'd been, and Mibu and the others followed suit.

"Now," said Jiro, "we'll have a good laugh when they come out."

The four of them, Jiro included, watched with interest to see when the door would open. It wavered a little, then closed again.

It was obvious they were huddling together, conferring on the best moment at which to emerge.

All of a sudden, the door burst open, and one of them dashed out. Mibu and his friends, their faces lined up above their seats, roared with laughter. Another burst out. This one slunk past with face studiously averted. The four roared with laughter. A short interval, and the last of them emerged, dawdling and tucking a colored handkerchief into his breast pocket as he came, managing with great effort to present an unconcerned profile as he passed. Once more, they exploded with laughter.

"What a great guy Kokubu is!" thought Mibu to himself.

Mibu had never had a really serious talk with Jiro, but on one occasion, when they came across each other by the flower beds in front of the library, he had asked him, his eye on a group of neighborhood children who were playing close to them:

"Do you want children, Kokubu-san?"

"Children? I haven't got around to thinking about it yet. I wonder . . . if I had a kid of my own would I be fond of it?"

"But surely you'll have children sooner or later?"

"Mm. I expect it would be fun."

"I wonder whether it'll be soon or in the distant future?"

Jiro's face just then seemed to lose a coating, as though a layer of silver foil had been stripped away by the wind. Without realizing it, Mibu had uttered the forbidden word.

"Human beings—," Mibu went on, "they go on being born and dying, dying and being born. It's kind of boring, isn't it?"

"Did you think that up yourself? Or did you read it somewhere?"

"No—the idea just kind of came to me, vaguely."

"Then you'd better drop it. Stop thinking about things in the future. You're too young for it."

"I'm young, yes—that's why I've got hopes for the future."

"Well, I have hopes too. But I haven't got time to think about trivial things." His tone conveyed utter rejection.

Watching him, Mibu had a breathtaking sense of the present as something ablaze before Jiro's eyes, a bright red ball that he stared at unwaveringly.

"I want to make myself as good at fencing as you."

"It's a matter of training," said Jiro. "Nothing matters but training."

5

The fencing club's summer training camp was to be held in Tago, a fishing village on the west coast of the Izu peninsula, for twelve days beginning on August 23. The mayor of Tago, an alumnus of the college, had helped with all kinds of arrangements.

They were to stay at the Enryuji, a Zen temple. The local Tago festival was on the twenty-first; once that was over and the overnight visitors from neighboring communities had gone home, the bonito boats began to put to sea, destined for the Bonins or as far afield as Saipan, and the town rapidly regained its placid air.

The Tago Song runs:

Oh, Izu has many harbors,
But come to Tago and see
The mountains of fish,
With Mt. Ima to the north
Facing the sunny south,
And the flowers blooming
In its terraced fields.

The town, trapped between two branches of the Nekko volcanic chain, has only five percent level land. The number of households is a little over a thousand at most.

The harbor, one of the finest on the Izu peninsula, is about a hundred and eighty feet deep at its mouth. There are twenty-four diesel boats for bonito and tuna fishing, and three steep-sided little islands near its entrance—Tagoshima, Takanoshima, and Bentenjima—give a pleasing variety to the view.

Besides fishing, the inhabitants also grow flowers on the slopes running down to the sea. Shipments of green peas are on the increase. But where the necessities of everyday life are concerned it relies entirely on outside supplies, and the club camp had to cook its own meals, one member being appointed each day to think out the menus and go around buying foodstuffs that would give the most nourishment at the cheapest possible prices.

The Enryuji stands away from the center of the town, up against the Otago hills on the other side of a tunnel. There is a newly built middle school nearby, with a fine gymnasium which was made available for daily fencing practice.

The party of thirty-eight boarded a boat at Numazu to take them along the west Izu coast to Tago. It was getting dark when they arrived, and that evening a welcome party was held for them at the temple by the mayor, with food that the mayor had had delivered specially. All-out training was due to begin the very next morning. The late summer heat was oppressive, and some of the club members had been looking forward to swimming, but they had barely arrived when Jiro put paid to any such hopes.

"Swimming," he declared uncompromisingly, "exercises the whole body, so you're to keep strictly away from the water, and that includes rest periods too. The rest periods are for resting, so you're not to take any exercise that would tire you for the training. We may be near the sea here, but for *you* the sea doesn't exist. If the sight of it bothers you, it means you still aren't putting enough into the training.

"And a special word to first-year members," he went on, "—you'd better stoke up on food at tonight's party. For three days starting tomorrow you're going to be too tired to have much appetite. Not that that's anything to worry about—you'll be eating properly again from the fourth day on."

As he delivered this pep talk to the club members in the temple's dimly lit main hall, where they had drifted, Jiro had a sudden recollection of something Kinouchi had said to him before they set out:

"You shouldn't drive the younger fellows quite so hard, you know. You might include a bit more in the way of recreation, for instance."

"Even so," Jiro had come back smartly, "I think it's wrong to spoil them."

He was not in the slightest shaken in his convictions. Beginning the next morning, they would go at it till they dropped. That was his job—to give them a taste of what lay beyond: the faint glimmerings of a physical awakening, a new sense of being uncluttered that came after pushing oneself to the limit. To Jiro himself, at least, it was all quite familiar.

"We're here to suffer, not to enjoy ourselves. Just bear that in mind!"

With these words, Jiro concluded his first address to them.

The morning of the first day at camp dawned.

The voice of the student on duty rang out over the thirty-eight forms lined up asleep on their quilts in the main hall:

"Everybody up!"

This being the first day, they were all keyed up, and there were no drowsy faces. There followed a confused rushing to and fro, the members stumbling over each other in an attempt to get their quilts put away and themselves washed in the prescribed ten minutes.

"You're disorganized—that's why it takes so long," shouted Jiro. "Half of you should put your bedding away before washing, the other half wash before tidying up. If only you do it in an orderly way, it takes no time. Mibu—get the shutters open!"

Mibu felt a tense pleasure, his spirit danced with a keen joy at being the first to be called on by Jiro on the first morning of camp. He flung himself at the hall's heavy wooden shutters, shoving them open to right and left. Beneath his eyes was revealed the sea—the forbidden sea—dazzling under the sun rising over the hills to the east.

"Get a move on!" bawled Jiro again. "That ten minutes is up already!"

A quarter of an hour later, the group finally started a fifteen-minute period of *seiza*, sitting formally on the tatami in the main hall.

At 6:30, the morning training session of about an hour began.

In training gear with pleated skirt and running shoes, they gathered in the temple's courtyard, which was full of the twittering of sparrows. The priest was not in evidence, but the area had already been scrupulously swept and even the tiniest shadow looked newly scrubbed.

Then they set out on a two-mile run. Down the stone steps, out onto the highway that ran by the sea.... Through the Otago tunnel, along the streets of Tago itself, and on as far as the other side of the tunnel that marked the southern extremity of the town.... That made approximately a mile, or two both ways.

71

The town, being a fishing port, was long since up and about. Today there must be boats setting sail for distant waters, as women, young and old together, were walking in the direction of the harbor.

"One, two! One, two!" As Jiro sang out the time for them, he was aware, out of the corner of his right eye, of the glitter of the sea that he himself had placed off limits.

It was hard work climbing the stone steps on the way back; but when they got back to the temple grounds Jiro, without pausing for rest, gave the order for warm-up exercises.

The exercises ended.

"Fetch the swords and form a circle!"

"Come on! At the double!"

The sun was already hot in the courtyard. They formed a ring and each of them did three to four hundred practice strokes, taking his time and counting from one to ten over and over again. Then, without a break, they did another hundred and fifty, this time as rapidly as possible.

Yamagishi, the manager, who normally took no part in training, wielded his bamboo sword alongside them. In Murata's mild, stolid face, the heavy eyelids looked still more sleepy now as he made his strokes. Kagawa, expressionless, simply went through the motions. Jiro, unlike the rest, stood correctly, his eyes fierce, bringing his sword whistling down through the morning air with grim determination. The pale triangle of bare chest showing between the lapels of his tunic, which opened and closed as he moved, shone with sweat as it caught the early morning sun.

Three dozen swords whirred through the air, and the cries of encouragement, taken up first by one then another, echoed in the hills behind the temple. Their mouths panted, their rib cages heaved and sank, their energy was expended pointlessly, it seemed, on the empty center of the circle that they formed.

The summer morning, the first hardships of full-time training, the breeze off the sea, the companionable rivalry—such clearly identifiable joys together with an almost dizzying excitement gradually mingled in an all-embracing fatigue. Now they heard nothing but the voices of three dozen swords being brought down into nothingness: the light, dry sound of bamboo, suggesting within it a certain luminosity like gold dust. Finishing his drill, Mibu was pleasantly aware of the emptiness of his mind as he awaited Jiro's next order.

Now came the fifty-yard sprint, for three or four of them at a time.

After this, they were told to make a circle again and do push-ups.

"Fifteen, sixteen, seventeen, eighteen . . ." Jiro's own breathing flogged them on as he counted.

Mibu noticed drops of his own sweat making black spots in the dry ocher soil of the yard. At first, the soil in contact with his hands had conveyed a sense of freshness, as though he were placing their imprint on something that no one had touched before, but as the number of times increased the earth changed into something hard and antagonistic, a malevolent force that pressed up from its own side against his palms.

"Twenty-five, twenty-six, twenty-seven, twenty-eight . . ."

A gouging pain afflicted him at the top of his arms, and he felt the sandy ground pushing up as though trying to bite him in the face. The black dots formed by his sweat grew there, only to dry up and vanish. One of the dots moved: it was an ant. It seemed incredible to him that an ant should be in such a place.

"Thirty-five, thirty-six, thirty-seven, thirty-eight . . ."

Glancing up, he saw that Yamagishi had already given up and

73

was hanging about by the entrance to the main hall as though he had some business there. Kagawa had quit too, and was giving encouragement to the younger men, his bamboo sword idle at his side.

"Forty-five, forty-six . . ."

By the time they had reached seventy, there were only some fifteen of them left, apart from Jiro himself.

Breakfast was at eight. The two junior students on duty were making hot bean-paste soup.

In the duty roster posted the previous evening, the tasks of cooking, cleaning, and fetching the milk had been allotted to first- and second-year students, with Mibu due to cook on the third day. Tomorrow, he would have to take over from the previous shift in going to buy provisions and planning the menu.

Sitting correctly on their heels, they said a brief grace in unison before taking up their chopsticks.

During the rest period of something over an hour that followed the meal Mibu had no energy even to raise his eyes and gaze out of the window at the sea. A stiff bout of fencing drill began at ten. Together, they changed into training uniforms with breastplates and thigh protectors over them, took up their face guards, gauntlets, and swords, and proceeded to the middle-school gymnasium.

The gym was new and well-appointed. The floor, though, unlike that of a proper fencing hall, lacked resilience and sent a dull ache through the heel that stamped on it.

Kokubu Jiro came out into the center of the gym to take charge of the camp's first fencing session.

In a clear, resounding voice he announced the beginning of training.

He gave the order for loosening-up exercises; when these

74

were over, he selected the older students who were to provide the opponents against whom the younger men pitted themselves, and had the whole group put on their masks, then begin the warm-up session: two hours of intense drill centered on strokes to the left and right of the opponent's head.

Jiro was familiar with every detail of the good qualities, failings, and idiosyncracies of each of the members. He could tell who was who even from afar, even if they were wearing masks and protectors. He himself would maintain a certain distance, keeping himself on the move so as to make the other move too. When a sagging sword tip told him that his partner was tiring, he would redouble his cries of encouragement, driving him on to the very limit of his strength and using every possible type of abuse to provoke his will to fight.

Jiro in the fencing hall was a god on the rampage; all the heat and energy of the training session seemed to emanate from him, to be transmitted in turn to his surroundings. No doubt, the heat and energy came from that sun that he had stared at as a boy.

It gave him assurance, too: who else could transform himself into such a graceful embodiment of assurance as Jiro in his element—the fencing hall? When he raised his sword straight above him before bringing it down on the other man's head, the conviction towered lofty and shining, overwhelming his opponent from the start.

In their brief rest breaks the first-year members would whisper to each other, between gasps for breath:

"Look at that—the way he's holding the sword over his head, it could split your skull open!"

When he raised it high for an attack, it loomed like a great menacing horn, and a disembodied vitality seemed to rise up above him like a column of cloud in the summer sky, full of radiant pride. The face guard gleamed and his weapon pointed to the heavens, at ease, looking down on its opponent. Then, as it descended, the sky was split in two so that it almost seemed to be the momentary cleft in the sky itself that fell on the victim's head.

However, in today's attack drill this dazzling set piece of Jiro's was not in evidence.

A mocking whirlwind, he reduced his opponents to exhaustion. Yet unlike Kagawa his movements followed a pattern, with none of Kagawa's sloppiness. At any given moment, the pose he assumed was correct, relaxed, natural. To the inexperienced members of the club as he took them on for practice, it seemed that there were any number of different Kokubu Jiros.

Cries, sweat, the thud of feet on the floor—from amidst the turmoil the thwack of the bamboo swords resounded like the bursting of a firecracker.

Great irregular waves rose and fell, enfolding within them the fencers' desperate breathing. It was a dark maelstrom of yells and leaping bodies, the whole resolving itself into one single call of the blood.

Jiro alone was aloof and untouched. Alone in this murky world he remained clear as crystal, so that the activity around him seemed almost a defilement.

Through the midst of this dark, thudding tumult he moved, too swift for the eye to notice, yet silent. And when he came to a sudden halt he was an ominous, dark blue, untouchable force temporarily held in check.

6

It was on the third day, when Mibu was on duty, that

everyone's fatigue reached a peak. During breaks, they had no energy even to talk.

Cruel heat and weariness bore down heavily on the young group. In the spacious temple kitchen, Mibu was nauseated by the smell of the curry that he and the other boy on duty were stirring.

For three days, training had continued remorselessly and without the slightest variation: two hours all-out from ten in the morning, devoted mainly to attack drills, another two hours beginning at three in the afternoon, and an hour's discussion to review the day from eight in the evening. Mibu could still hear Jiro's voice at the meeting:

"It's no good concentrating on hitting your opponents. The important thing is a correct stroke. The line of the sword has to be carried through. And you're getting up too close as well. . . ."

The arm that stirred the curry was heavy as lead; it was an effort just to stand.

In the temple living quarters, the voice of the priest, languidly repetitive, could be heard intoning the sutras.

Mibu looked down at his toes. The flesh between the big toe and the next was a bright, artificial red where it was painted with mercurochrome.

That morning, being on duty, he'd got up thirty minutes earlier than the others; now it was still before noon, but he was sleepy and yawned several times. Even so, part of his mind was worrying whether Jiro would be pleased with the curry or not. If by some word or other Jiro showed his approval, he'd be more than satisfied. He put in salt, then pepper, then took a taste, and added more curry powder. He tasted it again, and added some sugar. He had a feeling that the flavor had got muddled, like a painter's palette on which all kinds of colors had been mixed to produce a darkish mess.

In his diary for that day, he wrote:

August 26, fine.
On duty: Mibu, Maeda.
Members present in lodgings: 38.
Mail: Kuwano, Oikawa, Sasaki.
Expenses: ¥2,700
    Vegetables—¥1,600
    Meat—¥600
    Fish, etc.—¥500
Impressions: Hot again today, really hot! It's our job as
cooks to help the rest keep hard at it, which is quite a responsibility. The third day of hard training. According to the
captain, you don't get an appetite till the fourth, so I'm
unlucky to have got the day before. Still, they seemed to enjoy the curry I took such trouble over, so I'm pleased.

Mibu's entry made no reference to the fact that Jiro himself
had eaten in silence without a single comment as to whether he
enjoyed it or not.

With the fourth day, the camp entered on its middle phase
and the program became a little easier.

As the body grew exhausted, so the training itself became
familiar. As he had planned from the start, Jiro gradually cut out
those drills that could be omitted, with the addition of rotary
practice, and increased the number of practice matches, thus
lessening the pressure somewhat. This gave the others a sense
of confidence and pleasure, as though they'd reached the top of
a steep and trying climb and emerged onto a rather more level
stretch.

On the fifth day a cable came from Kinouchi in Tokyo. Something had turned up that would delay his arrival until the eighth day, instead of the sixth as scheduled. And since he expected to arrive by ship during the break after lunch, it wouldn't be necessary to go to meet him.

"He says he doesn't need meeting," said Jiro in front of the rest of them, "but we can't just leave it at that. Three of us— Yamagishi, Murata, and myself—will go to the harbor. He's sure to bring a whole load of things to eat and drink with him, so he'll need porters."

As he had predicted, the junior members had recovered their appetites, and there were whoops of joy at the idea of these contributions.

The eighth day arrived.

The camp was in its final stage, and most of their training was focused on practice matches. For the first time in many days, they had a chance to see Jiro demonstrate his authoritative sword-over-head stance.

His opponent was Murata.

Jiro raised his sword with both hands, high and tilted to the left. From between the sturdy arms crossing the front of his face guard, placid eyes, wide open and purged of all feeling, gazed at the other man.

The eyes seemed to want nothing. One wondered if he had *any* intense, overriding desires at all—apart, that is, from winning the all-Japan championship. . . .

Approaching ultimate perfection, bound fast by glory and honor, knowing that his prowess had become next to second nature, he nevertheless gave the impression of being sunk in a kind of torpor. Having created a world in which, all but selfless, he moved with perfect freedom, he still drove himself on relentlessly—with nothing to show for it but that quiet, utterly undemanding look.

Within the shadow of the mask, beneath sweat-drenched eyebrows, amidst the damp warmth of his own breath, the eyes were two crystals of frozen intellect. Neither the oiliness of the youthful face nor the odor of his clammy body could blur the tranquil light emanating from them, the composure so rapidly recovered from moment to moment. They were the eyes of a young fox spying an intruder from the depths of its lair.

The sword was held poised high above him at an angle. The strength supporting it bore it up buoyantly, so that it resembled the moon floating oblique in the early evening sky. He faced his opponent motionless, his body twisted, left foot advanced, right foot to the rear. As the black-lacquered breastplate inched around to meet the foe, it had a subdued luster and the light glinted on the sharp golden leaves that the gentian crest stretched out to right and left.

Thus did Kokubu Jiro become the embodiment of all that might or might not happen in the next moment, of all that unpredictable, tension-filled, silent world. It was at this point more than any other that he truly existed. He had become so because he had believed it *should* be so.

How could he bear, wondered Mibu with a sort of shudder, to live only in such isolated moments? Did he have anything to link them together?

Directing his sword toward the other's eyes, Murata slowly edged around to the left.

It felt as though the gym were hung with dark curtains, great dark curtains when the wind had dropped, leaving not a breath of air to stir it. In such an atmosphere, the heat was like the point of a silver needle.

Murata moved further to the left. As he did so, his body, try as it might to take up a different position while maintaining the same form, resisted in its various parts with the faintest, almost audible friction.

Toward that subtle lack of smoothness of movement, that faintest rasping as of sand, Jiro's sword came sweeping down in a great rush.

The sword hurtled down of its own volition, and as Jiro gave a yell Murata, whose attention had been directed entirely upward, felt it land on his breastplate with a clear-cut sound like a blow from a drumstick.

Mibu looked away with a feeling of relief; he couldn't have borne the tension of watching any more. And as he did so, his eye caught, below the gym's wide-open doors, the sharp, glinting line of the sea.

He recalled the first pep talk that Jiro had given: "If the sight of it bothers you, it means you still aren't putting enough into the training."

Kinouchi's boat was supposed to arrive at 1:00 P.M. The schedule was rather unreliable, and Jiro, Yamagishi, and Murata left the Enryuji together as soon as they had finished their midday meal, in case it was early.

The steamer wharf lay at the southern extremity of Otago Bay, just this side of the tunnel, a considerable distance to go on foot.

The rest were left behind in the hot, humid atmosphere of the main hall.

Not a breath of air stirred. The song of the cicadas pressed in on all sides.

Thirty-five club members lay draped about the hall, all but naked, in a variety of attitudes. Most were sprawled on the tatami, but some were seated in the windows and several sat in a circle playing cards. One of the windows was smothered by the leaves of a phoenix tree, translucent in the strong sunlight.

Sweat broke out on naked backs; here and there a round paper fan moved lethargically. Everywhere, the subtle play of light on young skin revealed undulations in the smooth flesh like the exposed roots of a tree.

The raised sanctuary enshrining the statue of the Buddha at the rear of the hall was buried in a daytime dusk through which golden accouterments and banners of gilt openwork gleamed faintly.

The young men had already tired of amusing themselves by defiantly hitting the "wooden fish" used to beat time during services. Even so, they were not, as they had been in the early days of the camp, prostrate with fatigue, too weary even to talk. They were lying like this to conserve their strength; yet under the surface there was a sullen pool of surplus energy.

Kagawa sat in a corner, propped against the paneled wall, surveying the others.

He acknowledged Jiro's ability in having dragged the camp along with him to this point. He admitted to himself, with a heavy spirit, Jiro's combination of forceful leadership and painstaking attention to detail.

He could hardly have said by now just what he had taken part in the camp for. It had been, of course, because he wanted to participate in the national championships, to brush up his technique as a regular. Yet to watch in silence, to go along with everything, was not really his kind of role. During his stay here he had, by stages imperceptible to himself, yielded to the intensity of Jiro's gaze, had given in to the beauty of that smile. And eight days were already past.

A spasm of anger made him suddenly want to burst out singing; but he knew no songs worth speaking of. So without warn-

ALMOST TRANSPARENT BLUE

Ryu Murakami/Translated by Nancy Andrew

"A Japanese mix of *A Clockwork Orange* and *L'Etranger.*"—*Newsweek*   128 pp; $5.95

THE AUTUMN WIND:
A Selection from the Poems of Issa

Translated and introduced by Lewis Mackenzie

A representative collection of classics from a haiku master.   146 pp; $4.95

THE BARREN ZONE

Toyoko Yamasaki/Translated by James T. Araki

After surviving several years in Siberian prisoner of war camps, a Japanese army officer returns to an unfamiliar Japan.   392 pp; available only in Japan

BETTY-SAN

Michiko Yamamoto
Translated by Geraldine Harcourt

"Impressive. The stories' rich sense of place weaves an unsentimental poetry from their loneliness."
—*Publishers Weekly*   152 pp; $4.95

BLACK RAIN

Masuji Ibuse/Translated by John Bester

A novel about Hiroshima.
"A painful and very beautiful book."—John Hersey
        300 pp; $6.95

BOTCHAN

Soseki Natsume/Translated by Alan Turney

The hilarious classic tale about a young man's rebellion.
"Soseki's lightest and funniest work."—Donald Keene   174 pp; $5.95

CHILDHOOD YEARS: A Mem

Jun'ichiro Tanizaki/Translated by Paul

"Invaluable as a guide to his derful portrait of
Review of Book

CHRONIC

Yasushi Inoue,

One of Japa
mother's last
"A gentle mer

A DARK N

Naoya Shiga/

A story of a
family.
"One of the g
ture."—*Choic*

THE DAR

Junnosuke Yo

Despite carryi
ship at a time,
love.
"The translat

THE DO

Sawako Ariyo
Translated by

A tender tale
well as a com
in Japanese s
"An excellent

ing he bellowed in a raucous voice:

"Hey—why don't we all go for a swim?"

Lazily, the young men sprawled on the floor raised their heads.

For a while, Kagawa's proposal failed to penetrate their heat-befuddled brains. Then one of them, as though suddenly waking up, shouted in an access of rebellious courage:

"Good idea! Come on, let's go!"

"The captain said not to."

"I know that."

"Then why suggest it?"

"Now's our chance," put in Kagawa with a sly grin. "Just leave it to me. I'm not so stupid as to let us get found out. The boat'll be late, for one thing. Just a quick dip, and we'll feel better. There'll be nobody watching in a bay like this. We can come back, wash off, and behave as though nothing happened. It's a shame when the sea's right there in front of our noses. Getting a bit wet isn't going to interfere with training, I promise you. Come on, then—we won't get another chance. I *know* you all want to swim. You don't need to tell me!"

"We don't have any swimming trunks."

"You can wear your underpants, can't you? It isn't a beach resort."

Watching their reactions, Kagawa felt a thrill of pleasure. Unlike an order from Jiro, his suggestion caused confusion at first, a tingling, not unpleasant pricking of the conscience, followed by fear and vacillation, which prompted in turn the courage to shake these off and charge ahead.

"Let's go! What are we hanging around for!"

With a slap at his bare chest he stood up, experiencing at that moment a burst of something close to friendship for Jiro. What he was doing was entirely for his sake. He couldn't care less about the rest of them. In his own mind, he was invoking Jiro almost constantly: *Don't get me wrong: this is a sign of friendship. You're convinced that nobody understands you, but there are situations where even you can't help getting other people wrong yourself. Anyway, you need to be startled and threatened by something. That's the thing you need to be taught above everything else.*

The others were getting up, then sitting down again, keeping a careful eye on Kagawa and arguing among themselves in a buzz of voices. The urge to go down to the sea and swim raced around among them like a Chinese firecracker: they leaped in fear of getting burned, they ran away only to be drawn close again.

Kagawa watched them as a man watches a pond full of pet carp. He had given them food; now, squabbling though they were, their ultimate object was the same.

"Right, then," he said lightly, confirming what no longer needed confirmation. The group stood up, revealing Mibu still sprawled alone on the floor behind them.

"What's up? Got a bellyache or something?"

"No. I'm staying here."

As he replied, Mibu raised himself hastily and sat stiffly upright. His eyes were blazing with anger. Kagawa could see Jiro in them.

"OK. Suit yourself."

And he made a gesture that even he found rather overdone. Leaning his body to one side, and with a broad sweep of the arm on the other side in the manner of a cheerleader at a ball game, he set off running for the exit, ahead of the others. Directly beneath his gaze stretched the glittering waters of Otago Bay, and beyond them an immense, forbidding horizon lay burdened with heavy summer clouds.

Bare to the waist, the young men came bounding after him down the stone steps of the temple, cut across the white, empty highway with a shout, and scattered over the hot, deserted sands of the bay.

Left on his own, Mibu was quivering with anger.

He no longer had eyes for the sea; he was thinking exclusively of Jiro. Seated like this, alone and in formal fashion, he felt once more the pain he'd had to bear before on Jiro's account. A finger's breadth of sunlight shone through the window of the main hall and fell burning onto the tatami. He wished he were that tatami, baking in the sun.

Time passed. Yet how slowly it passed! Sharp within himself he could feel the pain of Jiro's wounded pride. Never in his life so far, he thought, had be felt another's pain so vividly.

His ears were stuffed with the sound of the cicadas. He felt a single-minded hatred, but it was not for Kagawa personally. In it, he seemed to detect something immense and—strange though the word might seem—public. Far from constricting his mind, it seemed to broaden it immeasurably, almost to tear it apart.

Something strong and just and serene had been defiled. What had taken place was awful, intolerable; but he felt at the same time that he had foreseen it all along.

Exactly what had happened? He put the question to himself again. Simply that the others had gone for a swim while the captain was away. That was all. And yet it had been enough to make something collapse—collapse once and for all.

The sweat dripped from his forehead and ran down his cheeks. It welled at his throat and flowed down his chest. An inexhaustible reservoir of sweat. . . . If only, he thought, everything were inexhaustible in this way—his sweat, his emotions, his sincerity—he would hardly need to exist as an independent, solid entity. It would be enough to be connected up with something, to be connected to the source of the stream. He'd been sure of that so far; but sources dwindle and dry up, and the more he sought to cling to them the farther, he suspected, they would recede into the distance.

His knee was moist with sweat, and a fly came and settled there. The fly sucked greedily at the sweat, sucked at his pores. He would just have to put up with it; if you couldn't bear even one single thing through to the end, then you might as well give up entirely.

At that moment, far off, he heard a car's horn, an unusual sound in these parts, and was on his feet before he realized it.

Between the trees, a car traveling along the highway from the direction of the town could be seen turning into the road that led around and up the slope to the back entrance. It was the mayor's car. After eight days, his shiny black Toyopet was familiar to all the club members.

Suddenly, the truth struck him. The mayor must have heard about Kinouchi's arrival and sent his car to the harbor to meet him.

The Enryuji could be reached, not just by climbing straight up the stone steps from the highway, but also by car, by the road that went around the long way to the back of the temple. The only reason few people took the detour was that it was too far on foot.

Mibu's heart began to beat faster.

The swimmers, unaware of the danger, had not returned yet.

The boat must have been early. That, together with the fact that they'd come by car, was what had upset the schedule in this way.

Seeing himself as he would appear to them, sitting there alone in the hall when the car finally arrived and Kinouchi and Jiro came in, he felt the intense emotion he'd been experiencing collapse like a pricked balloon. The vision, with its reversal of appearance and intention, was acutely unpleasant. His sitting there would look like an empty form, a kind of placard. . . . It would seem to be the thing he most despised: showy hypocrisy. Even if he had originally decided to behave as he had for Jiro's sake, he would rather die than have Jiro see him do it.

No sooner did he feel this than he had slipped on a pair of straw sandals and was running away from the main building.

Then, as though to confirm the danger, he peered out from behind a tree toward the rear entrance. From here it was possible, while keeping out of sight behind the trees, to flee in the direction of the stone steps at the main entrance without being spotted by visitors at the rear.

The growl of the car drew nearer. It had just reached the top of the slope. It stopped. A door opened and Murata got out of the seat next to the driver while Jiro alighted from the rear carrying a large bundle in his arms. They stood with their backs to him, watching Kinouchi get out.

Seized with an impulse he didn't understand himself, Mibu spun around, raced toward the main gate, and ran down the steps. He must let the swimmers know immediately: the sense of duty drove him on, pressed at him strongly from behind. Why, he didn't know. But he wanted to be one of them as soon as possible, to blend in with the others' guilt.

It happened that just then the rest of them, having stopped swimming at what they thought was the right time, were coming back from the beach across the highway, with Kagawa at their head. Hell, thought Mibu, I'm the only one in dry pants; but nobody'll notice if I mix in with them. Driven by an odd eagerness to be punished just as soon as possible, he made straight for the approaching, sea-drenched figures.

Kinouchi had been there only a short while when the members of the club, still half-naked and wet, arrived back at the temple. Their chests were heaving from hurrying up the steps.

They greeted Kinouchi with silent bows; nobody ventured to speak. Summoning up his courage, one of them stepped up into the hall and sat down, and the rest trooped after him.

A long, hot silence ensued. Kinouchi was fanning himself, the only one to do so.

"This is some camp!" he said. "So you think you're the swimming club, do you?"

Getting no reply, he turned to Jiro.

"Did you give them permission to swim?"

Jiro, who had been staring at the floor, lifted his head at last and replied crisply,

"No, I didn't. It's my responsibility. I'm sorry."

Gazing from a distance at Jiro's tense look and flushed cheeks, Mibu, safe among his dripping fellows, was glad that his true intention remained unknown to Jiro, that he was holding himself suitably apart.

"I took them," said Kagawa, almost stammering.

"Why?"

"It was hot. . . . I thought they'd be glad of a dip."

"I see." Kinouchi fanned himself in silence for some time. "I see. . . . Kagawa—you're to go back to Tokyo today. That's an order. You don't have to worry—Kokubu and I can take charge for the remaining two days. . . . But training camp and actual matches are two different things. Mind you don't forget you're still a regular member of the team. When you get home, do your thousand practice strokes every day; that should be enough to keep someone like you in shape. Anyway, off you go today."

"Very well, sir."

As he spoke Kagawa gave Jiro a fierce stare. It was clearly apparent to Mibu even at a distance. Jiro's head was hanging, his eyes fixed on the floor, his appearance almost wilting, as though he were beside himself with shame. To Mibu it seemed as if Jiro's proud gaze had transferred itself to Kagawa.

No one was punished save Kagawa; the ordinary members heard nothing more of the affair. Among the junior students the view was that Kagawa—who had never been popular—had overstepped the mark in trying to get himself liked. There was little sympathy for him. The afternoon boat left while they were all at training, and nobody went to the harbor to see him off.

After the evening meal, Mibu, stepping out into the darkness of the temple garden to get some cool air, saw Jiro standing by the steps at the main gateway.

It was a starry night; the heat of the day lingered in the trees and undergrowth round about, though the air was full of the night song of insects.

Mibu was wondering whether to go nearer or not when Jiro himself called out:

"Hey—Mibu."

It was too dark to see his face properly.

"Yes?"

Jiro started to say something, then seemed to hesitate for a while.

"Look, Mibu—," he said, calling the other by his name again, "did you go to the beach with the rest of them?"

Mibu now found himself obliged to make a decision that he'd known he would have to face sooner or later. He was being required to state, before Jiro, whether he was really himself, Mibu, or not. It was an agonizing problem: if he wanted to be himself, it meant telling a lie. He gazed at Jiro in distress. But the look was lost, futile, in the darkness; he felt he was back in the training hall, felt again the aimlessness of his sword tip, left in the air as his attack was diverted.

"Yes," he said.

"You really went," Jiro pressed. At that moment, Mibu stood poised on the threshold of the calm authority that he had learned from Jiro himself.

"Yes," he replied cheerfully. He had the feeling that for the first time he had made chest-to-chest contact with Jiro, that for the first time his own stature had measured up to his.

7

The party on September 2 to mark the end of their training camp was a lively affair. For the first time they were allowed to drink and smoke; Kinouchi did his imitations of a cat and a dog howling, and they sang the college song in chorus, along with a dubious version of a popular song of the Meiji period.

Jiro, who didn't drink, made no mention of the swimming episode in his speech at the beginning of the party, but praised their perseverance and fighting spirit.

"You've all done very well. Looking at your faces now, on this last evening, I feel you're somehow different people from ten days ago. A man's face changes after he's given all he has for some purpose. As I see it, our college can't help winning the championship—I think Mr. Kinouchi would agree. But the most dangerous thing is the feeling that now camp's over you deserve to take things easy. How to make this peak of condition, this peak readiness last until the national championships—that's the thing I'd like you to concentrate on from now on."

The speech, as goes without saying, earned an ovation, but

Mibu found it rather too tame, too run-of-the-mill for someone like Jiro.

The entertainment was still going on. People were still doing their party pieces when Jiro disappeared. A club member reported having seen him go out in his training tunic, with breastplate and thigh protectors, carrying his bamboo sword.

Jiro often went off by himself like that, to practice solo. The urge, it seemed, took hold of him whenever he suspected some kind of spiritual slackening in himself, some descent to the ordinary level of the spirit that he always kept keyed up beyond the average.

None of them gave much thought to the matter, but when with the approach of midnight Kinouchi declared the party over and they set about belated preparations for bed, Jiro still wasn't back, and there was a sudden commotion. Since he didn't drink, there was no chance that he had passed out somewhere on his own.

At Kinouchi's command they split up into three parties, each entrusted with one of the only flashlights available, and set off to search the temple grounds, the hill behind, and down to the beach.

"Kokubu-saan. Kokubu-saan." As first one group then another called, their voices grew progressively uneasier.

After about an hour's search, the party that included Mibu sighted Jiro in the woods at the top of the hill behind the temple. In the ray of their flashlight, they caught the gleam of his black-lacquered breastplate and the golden glimmer of the twin-leafed gentian crest.

His sword tucked beneath the arm of his uniform, Jiro lay on the ground, face up, dead.

SEA
AND
SUNSET

It was late summer in the ninth year of the Bunei era. It should be added here, since it will be important later, that the ninth year of Bunei is 1272 by Western reckoning.

An elderly man and a boy were climbing the hill known as Sho-jo-ga-take that lies behind the Kenchoji temple in Kamakura. Even during the summer, the man, a handyman at the temple, liked to get the cleaning done in the middle of the day, then, whenever there promised to be a beautiful sunset, to climb to the top of this hill.

The boy was deaf and dumb, and the village children who came to play at the temple always left him out of their games, so the old man, feeling sorry for him, had brought him up there with him.

The old man's name was Anri. He was not very tall, but his eyes were a clear blue. With his large nose and his deep eye sockets, his appearance was different from ordinary people; so the village brats were accustomed to calling him, behind his back, not Anri but "the long-nosed goblin."

There was nothing at all odd about his Japanese, nor had he any perceptible foreign accent. It was between twenty and twenty-five years since he had arrived here with the Zen Master Daigaku who had founded the temple.

The summer sunlight was beginning to slant its rays, and the area around the Shodo that was sheltered from the sun by the hills was already in shadow. The main gate of the temple reached up to the sky as though marking the boundary between day and night. It was the hour when the whole temple compound, with its many clumps of trees, was suddenly overtaken by shade.

Yet the west side of Shojo-ga-take, up which Anri and the boy were climbing, was still bathed in strong sunlight and the cicadas were clamorous in its woods. Amidst the grasses that gave off a summery odor beside the path, a few crimson spider lilies gave notice of the approach of autumn.

Arrived at the summit, the two of them left their sweat to dry in the cooling breeze off the hills.

Below them the sub-temples making up the Kenchoji lay spread out for their inspection: Sairaiin, Dokeiin, Myokoin, Hojuin, Tengenin, Ryuhoin. . . . Hard by the main gate, a young juniper tree that the founder had brought as a sapling from his home in Sung China was clearly discernible, gathering the late summer sun to itself on its leaves.

Directly below them on the slope of Shojo-ga-take itself, the roof of the Okunoin was visible, and below it again rose the roof of the belfry. Beneath the cave where the Master had practiced meditation, a grove of cherry trees which in season would become a sea of blossom formed a shady retreat of rich green foliage. At the foot of the hill, Daigaku Pond announced its presence with a dull glint of water through the trees.

But it was at something other than these features of the scene that Anri was gazing.

It was the sea, glittering in a distant line beyond the rise and fall of Kamakura's hills and valleys. Throughout the summer one could, from here, watch the sun sink into the sea in the vicinity of Inamura-ga-saki.

Near where the dark blue of the horizon touched the sky lay a low line of cumulus clouds. It did not move, but like a morning glory slowly unfurling its petals was drifting open, gradually changing shape. The sky above it was a clear yet somewhat faded blue, and the clouds, though not colored as yet, seemed brushed with the faintest tinge of peach by a light coming from within.

The state of the sky showed summer and autumn just coming to terms with each other: for high up, way above the horizon, mackerel clouds stretched across it in a band, a fleecy mass that spread a softly mottled pattern over Kamakura's many valleys.

"Why, they're just like a flock of sheep," said Anri in a voice hoarse with age. But the boy, being deaf and dumb, simply sat there on a nearby rock, gazing intently up at him. Anri might have been talking to himself.

The boy could hear nothing—his mind comprehended nothing—yet his limpid gaze suggested an infinite wisdom, so that it seemed that the feeling Anri wanted to convey, if not his words, might be transmitted directly from Anri's clear blue eyes to the boy's.

Which was why Anri spoke exactly as though he were addressing the boy. His words were not the Japanese of which he normally showed such a fluent command. They were French, a French interlarded with the dialect of the mountainous region in the south where he was born. If any of the other brats had heard him, they would have felt that this smoothly tripping, many-voweled speech came oddly from the lips of a goblin.

"Yes, just like a flock of sheep. . . ," repeated Anri, with a sigh this time. "I wonder what happened to those sweet little lambs of the Cévennes? By now, I expect, they've had children, and grandchildren, and great-grandchildren, then died themselves. . . ."

He lowered himself onto a rock, choosing a place where the summer grasses did not shut off the view of the distant sea.

The hillsides were full of singing cicadas.

Turning his azure eyes in the boy's direction, Anri spoke again.

"I'm sure you don't know what I'm saying. But you are different from those village people—you will probably believe me. It may be difficult, even for you, to accept. But hear it, just the same—no one apart from you is likely to take my story seriously. . . ."

He spoke haltingly. Whenever he got stuck, he made an odd, unfamiliar gesture as though to help summon up the next part of his tale.

". . . A long time ago, when I was around the same age as you are now—no, long before I was your age—I was a shepherd in the Cévennes. The Cévennes is the beautiful southern mountain area of France, the domain of the Count of Toulouse, the area south of Mt. Pilat. I don't suppose that means much to you—after all, the people of this country don't even know the name of my native land!

"It was around the year 1212, a time when the Fifth Crusade had for a while regained control of the Holy Land, only to see it snatched away once more. The French were sunk in grief, their womenfolk in mourning yet again.

"At dusk one day, I was driving my flock home from the pastures and had started to climb a small hill. The sky was almost unnaturally clear. The dog I had with me gave a low growl, dropped his tail, and behaved as though trying to hide behind me.

"Just then, I saw Christ in a shining white robe coming down the hill in my direction. He had a beard, just as he has in pictures, and his face wore a smile of infinite compassion. I prostrated myself. The Lord stretched out a hand and, I seem to remember, touched my hair. Then he said: 'It is thou, Henri, who shalt take back the Holy Land. Thou and other children like thee shall regain Jerusalem from the heathen Turk. Gather thy fellows, in great numbers, and betake thee to Marseilles. There, the waters shall be divided in two that thou mayst pass beyond, and to the Holy Land.'

". . . That much I heard, no mistake about it. For the rest, I was in a swoon. The dog licked my face to wake me, and when I came to it was there, right in front of me, peering anxiously into my face in the twilight. My whole body was bathed in sweat.

"When I got home I spoke to no one of what had happened: I felt that no one would believe me.

"It was four or five days later, a day of rain. I was alone in the shepherds' hut. Around dusk, just as before, there came a knock at the door. Going out, I found an aged traveler, who begged some bread of me. I stared intently at him. It was a solemn visage, with a large, high-bridged nose and white whiskers framing the face. The eyes, especially, had an almost frightening clarity. I bade him come in, as it was raining, but he made no answer. Then I saw that, though he had been walking through the rain, his robe was quite dry.

"I stood there awestruck, unable to speak. The old man thanked me for the bread and took his leave. As he went, I heard a voice say quite clearly in my ear: 'Hast thou forgotten the prophesy made a while since? Why dost thou hesitate? Knowst thou not that thou art entrusted with a mission by the Lord?'

"I made to go after the old man. But it was pitch dark all about, the rain was beating down, and the traveler was nowhere to be seen. The sound of the sheep bleating uneasily as they huddled together came to me through the rain. . . .

"I could not sleep that night.

"The next day, when I went out into the pastures, I finally told the story to a young shepherd of my own age with whom I

99

was particularly friendly. A pious youth, he no sooner heard my tale than he fell to his knees in the clover and paid homage to me.

"Within a week or so, I had collected a following among the shepherds of the neighborhood. I had no sense of self-importance, but they came forward of their own accord to be my followers.

"Before long, a rumor got about that an eight-year-old prophet had put in an appearance at a place not far from the village where I lived. The infant seer—so the stories said—was preaching and performing miracles; it was even said that he had laid hands on a blind girl and restored her sight.

"My followers and I went there to see for ourselves. We found the prophet playing and laughing merrily amid the other children. I went down on my knees before him, and told him in detail of the revelation.

"The child had a milky white complexion, and golden curls hung down over a forehead in which the blue veins were visible. As I knelt, he checked his laughter and his small mouth twitched two or three times at the corners. But it was not I he was looking at. He was gazing abstractedly at the meadows' undulating skyline.

"So I too looked in the same direction and saw, standing there, a rather tall olive tree. The light was filtering through its upper foliage, so that branches and leaves seemed to be glowing from within.

"A breeze swept across the land. Placing a solemn hand on my shoulder, the child pointed in that direction. And in the higher branches of the tree I saw quite clearly a host of angels, all moving their wings.

" 'You are to go east,' said the child in a voice entirely different in its solemnity from a moment before. 'Go east, and keep going. You had best go to Marseilles, as the revelation told you.'

"Thus the rumors spread. Similar things had been happening all over France. One day, the son of a man killed in the Crusades had taken up the sword his father had bequeathed him and left home. At another place, a child who had been playing by the fountain in the garden abruptly threw down his toys and went off, taking nothing but a piece of bread the maid had given him. When his mother caught and scolded him, he would not listen, but declared that he was going to Marseilles.

"In one village the children, slipping out of bed in the night, gathered in the village square, then set out for they knew not where, singing hymns as they went. When the grown-ups awoke, the village was bereft of all children save those who were still too small to walk.

"I myself was preparing to leave for Marseilles together with a large company of followers when my parents came to take me home, begging me in tears to give up my wild scheme. But my companions were impatient with such lack of faith and drove them off. Those who set out with me numbered, alone, no less than a hundred; in all, several thousand children from all over France and Germany were taking part in this Crusade.

"The journey was not easy. We had barely gone half a day when the youngest and the weakest began to fall by the way. We buried their bodies and wept, and set up small crosses of wood to mark the spots.

"Another company of a hundred children, I heard, strayed unwittingly into an area where the Black Death was rampant, and died, to the last child. One of our own band, a girl, was made delirious by fatigue and flung herself from a cliff.

"Strangely enough, these children as they died invariably had a vision of the Holy Land: a vision, I'm sure, not of the desolate

Holy Land of today, but a fertile place where the lilies bloomed in profusion, a plain flowing with milk and honey.... You may wonder how we knew such things, but some of them described their visions as they died, and even when they didn't their look was ecstatic, as though they were confronting vast realms of light. ...

"Well: we arrived in Marseilles.

"Scores of boys and girls were there before us, waiting in the hope that the waters of the sea would part when we appeared. Our number had already been reduced to a third by then.

"Surrounded by children with faces alight with anticipation, I went down to the harbor. There, amidst the rows of masts, the sailors gazed at us curiously. Reaching the quayside, I prayed. The sun was dazzling on the late afternoon sea. I prayed for a long time. The sea brimmed with water as ever, the waves beat heedless against the wharf.

"But we did not despair: the Lord was surely waiting till we were all assembled.

"A few at a time, the children arrived. All were exhausted, some grievously sick. Day after day we waited in vain; but the waters did not part.

"It was then that a man with an exceedingly pious air approached and gave us alms. Having done so, he offered, hesitantly enough, to take us to Jerusalem in his own ship. Half our number were reluctant to embark with him, but the other half, myself included, boldly went on board.

"The ship did not go to the Holy Land, but pointed its prow to the south and sailed till it reached Alexandria in Egypt. There, in the slave market, every one of us was sold."

Anri was silent for a while, as though recalling once more the anguish of that time.

Up in the sky a resplendent late-summer sunset had begun.

102

The mackerel clouds were all crimson, and there were other clouds too, as though long red and yellow streamers had been drawn across the sky. Out at sea, the heavens were like a fiercely blazing furnace.

The very grass and trees about them shone to a still brighter green in the sky's reflected flames.

By now Anri's words were aimed directly at the sunset, almost as if appealing to it. In the flames over the sea his eyes could make out the sights of his home, and the faces of its people. He could see himself as a boy. He could see the other shepherd boys, his friends. On hot summer days they would push their robes of rough cloth off their shoulders, revealing the rosy nipples on the fair-skinned, boyish chests. The faces of the young comrades who had been killed, or had died, rose up in a host in the sunset glow of the sea. They were bareheaded, yet their flaxen hair shone like helmets of fire.

Even when they survived, the boys and girls were scattered to the four quarters. Not once in all his long life as a slave did Anri come across a face he knew. He was never, in the end, to visit the Jerusalem he had so longed to see.

He became the slave of a Persian merchant. Sold a second time, he went to India. There, he heard rumors of a conquest of the West by Batu, grandson of Genghis Khan; and he wept at the peril facing his homeland.

In those days the Zen Master Daigaku was in India studying Buddhism. By a chance chain of circumstances, Anri was freed through the Master's aid. As a way of showing his gratitude, he determined that he would serve the Master for the remainder of his life. He followed him back to his own country, then, hearing that he was going over to Japan, made bold to request that he be allowed to accompany him there. . . .

Anri was at peace with himself by now. The vain hope of

103

returning home long since relinquished, he was resigned to laying his bones to rest in Japan. He had taken in the Master's teachings well, and never indulged in foolish fantasies of an afterlife or hankered after unseen lands. And yet when sunset colored the summer sky and the sea was a shining bar of scarlet, his legs seemed to start walking of their own accord, taking him irresistibly to the top of Shojo-ga-take.

He would watch the sunset, and the reflection on the waves; and irresistibly he would find himself recalling the wondrous things that just once—he was sure—had befallen him in the days when his life was still new. Once more, he would rehearse them to himself: the miracle; the yearning for the unknown; the strange force that had driven them to Marseilles. And, last of all, he would think of the sea and how, when he had prayed on the quayside of Marseilles in a crowd of children, it had not parted to let them pass but had gone on sending in its placid waves, glittering beneath the setting sun.

Just when he had lost his faith Anri could not remember. The one thing he could recall, vividly even now, was the mystery of the sea, aglow in the sunset, whose waters had failed to give way however much they prayed: a fact more incomprehensible than any miraculous vision. The mystery of that encounter between a boyish mind that saw nothing strange in a vision of Christ, and a sunset sea that refused absolutely to divide. . . .

If at any time in his life the sea had been going to part, it should have done so at that moment, yet even then it had stretched silent, fiery still in the sunset: there lay the mystery. . . .

Silent now, the old man from the temple stood there, the light glowing on his disheveled white hair and planting spots of scarlet in the clear azure of his eyes.

The late summer sun was beginning to sink off the coast of Inamura-ga-saki. The surrounding sea turned to a tide of blood.

He remembered the past, remembered the scenes and the people of his home. But now there was no desire to go back; for all of them—the Cévennes, the sheep, his native land—had vanished into the sunset sea. They had vanished, one and all, when the waves had refused to give way.

Anri, though, kept his eyes on the sunset as it changed color from moment to moment, consuming itself little by little and turning to ash.

The trees and plants of Shojo-ga-take, finally overtaken by shadow, showed all the more clearly the veins of their leaves and the contours of the knots in the wood. Some of the many lesser temple buildings were already sunk in the dusk.

The shadows were creeping up around Anri's feet; the sky above had drained to a dark, grayish blue. A glitter still lingered far offshore, but it had been squeezed by the dusky sky into a thin strip of gold and vermilion.

Just then, from below Anri as he lingered, there rose the deep boom of a temple bell; the belfry on the slope of the hill had begun to toll the end of day.

The sound of the bell came in slow waves that seemed to awake pulsations in the darkness, spreading it out in all directions. The gravely swaying sound did not so much tell the time as instantly dissolve it and carry it away into eternity.

Anri listened, his eyes closed. When he opened them again, he was submerged in dusk and the sea's distant border showed dim and ashen. The sunset was over.

Anri turned to the boy to suggest that they start back for the temple. The boy sat with arms clasped about his knees, on which his head rested. He was fast asleep.

CIGARETTE

I cannot look back on the turmoil of adolescence as something either enjoyable or attractive. "My youth was but a shadowy storm," writes Baudelaire in a poem, "shot through here and there by shafts of sunlight."

It's odd how one's memories of youth turn out so bleak. Why does the business of growing up—one's recollections of growth itself—have to be so tragic? I still haven't found the answer. I doubt if anybody has. When I finally reach that stage at which the placid wisdom of old age, with the dry clarity that comes toward autumn's end, occasionally descends on a person, then I too may suddenly discover that I understand. But I doubt whether, by that time, understanding will have much point.

Day follows day, nothing is ever really resolved: in adolescence, even this perfectly ordinary fact of life can seem intolerable. The adolescent has abandoned the clever ambiguity, the self-serving compromises of the very young. He finds them distasteful, and is disposed to start afresh, from the beginning. Yet how coldly the world views this fresh start! Not a soul is there to see him off when he sets sail. Again and again, people handle him the wrong way. One moment he's treated as an adult, the next as a child. Is it because there's nothing about him he can truly call his own? No—as I see it, adolescence has its own certainties which one would seek in vain elsewhere, and which the adolescent struggles to give a name to.

One day, however, he at last finds a name for them: "growing up." This achievement settles him, makes him proud. Yet the minute he identifies them, the certainties change into something different from what they were when they had no name. What's more, he becomes unable even to perceive this fact. In short, he becomes an adult. . . .

Held in the custody of childhood is a locked chest; the adolescent, by one means or another, tries to open it. The chest is opened: inside, there is nothing. So he reaches a conclusion: the treasure chest is always like this, empty. From this point on, he gives priority to this assumption of his rather than to reality. In other words, he is now a "grown-up." Yet was the chest really empty? Wasn't there something vital, something invisible to the eye, that got away at the very moment it was opened?

For me, at any rate, the process of becoming an adult refused to feel like any kind of self-fulfillment, or graduation. Boyhood, I believed, was something that should continue forever (and doesn't it in fact continue?). Why, then, should one have to treat it with contempt?. . .

From the outset of adolescence I couldn't, for one thing, bring myself to believe in "comradeship." My contemporaries seemed to me all insufferably dim. We were condemned to spend the greater part of our daylight hours at school—a stupid organization that obliged us to select friends from among a few dozen predetermined, boring boys of the same age. Within those confining walls, teachers—a bunch of men all armed with the same information—gave the same lectures every year from the same notebooks and every year at the same point in the textbooks made the same jokes. . . . (I and a friend in form B arranged between us to see how long after the start of a class it took a certain chemistry teacher to make his joke. In my class, it came in twenty-five minutes. In his, it came at 11:35, which was precisely the same amount of time.) What was I supposed to learn in this sort of framework?

Worse still, the adults demanded that everything we absorbed within those confines should be "worthwhile." So, quite naturally, we learned the alchemist's way of faking things, creating from lead a spurious substance which we persuaded our patrons was gold till, in the end, we were convinced ourselves that we'd produced the precious metal. It was the school's cleverest alchemist who earned the label of model student. The "model student," indeed, is one of the most accomplished frauds in any field.

I grew to loathe every single classmate of mine. Consciously, for its own sake, I began to do the reverse of everything they did. On entering middle school we were all supposed to take up some sport: I, inevitably, despised all games.

The older boys tried to force me into a sports club. I lied valiantly, stealing glances all the while at their brawny arms:

"I . . . you see . . . I've got weak lungs. And besides . . . you see . . . my heart's not strong, and sometimes I pass out."

One of them, his cap at a rakish angle and the hooks on the jacket of his uniform undone halfway down his chest, snorted in contempt:

"I suppose you realize you're not going to live very long with a pasty face like that? If you die now, you'll die without knowing what real fun is. Fun, get it? *Fun. . . .*"

My classmates, standing tense-faced around me in a ring, snickered suggestively. Without replying, I took another good look at the sturdy arms visible beneath the older boy's rolled-up sleeves. And, dimly enough as yet, I had an intimation of women as something intensely unattractive.

I resisted at every turn the oddly prurient atmosphere—that peculiar atmosphere so hard to convey to others—prevailing at the Peers' School, though there was something, lurking farther in the background, that I was thoroughly obsessed with. Most of my schoolmates had the kind of faces that, among normal people, would have been conspicuous for a combination of the supercilious and the faintly sinister. They rarely read books, and seemed almost proud of their extraordinary ignorance. They gave the impression of being immune to anything even remotely tragic. Immature though they were, they had the knack of steering clear of suffering, strong excitement, or any of the more overwhelming emotions. If, unavoidably, they'd been thrust into the midst of suffering, their very inertness would promptly have overcome it, and quite effortlessly they would have settled down to a life of indifference. They were the scions of a certain breed of men: men who have succeeded in subjecting large numbers of humanity not through intimidation or violence but by the sheer paralyzing power of inaction.

I was fond of walking in the broad stretch of undulating woodland that surrounded the school. Most of the school buildings stood on a piece of high ground whose slopes were thickly covered with trees and threaded by a number of treacherously slippery paths. Scattered among the trees, dismal and marshy, lay a series of ponds; it was as though the subterranean waters of the woods had gathered there hoping for a glimpse of the blue sky, and were taking a rest before returning to the darkness underground. If you looked, you could see that the heavy gray pools, seemingly immobile, were furtively and silently revolving. This secret activity of the marsh water held a constant fascination for me.

One day, perched on a rotting tree stump beside a pond, I sat gazing dreamily at the surface of the water, where fallen leaves drifted silently and almost imperceptibly. The incisive sound of an axe felling trees echoed somewhere deep in the woods. Just then, the restless autumn sky revealed a pool of blue that sent down a few rays of light from the edges of majestically gleaming clouds, and for a moment the sharp sound of the axe might have been the sound of light itself. Where the rays pierced them, the opaque waters of the marsh acquired a gold-tinged translucence, through which a single dead leaf sank glittering, turning over and over as it went like some sluggish pond creature. Watching it go, I had a sudden, unreasoning sense of happiness. For a short while, I felt that I'd at last become one with that great stillness with which I always longed to merge—that well-remembered stillness, inevitably spoiled by a host of irrelevancies, which seemed to emanate from some previous life.

I started off along the path around the edge of the pond, heading toward a hummock resembling an ancient burial mound that lay deep in the woods. Unexpectedly, though, I heard among the trees a sound like the rustling of bamboo grass. Two boys who had been lying sprawled in a small grassy clearing had sat up and were looking in my direction. They were older than me, strangers, and were obviously there, away from the eyes of the teaching staff, for the forbidden purpose of smoking.

After a hard look at me, one of them raised the cigarette he'd been cupping in his palm to his mouth. The other, with a rapid glance at the hand he'd been holding behind his back, gave an exclamation of annoyance.

"What's up? Have you let it go out?" jeered the first. "You silly idiot!"

He laughed heartily, to show he wasn't particularly bothered by my presence, but the laugh ended by making him choke on the unfamiliar tobacco smoke. The object of his mirth, a trifle pink about the ears, was ostentatiously going through the motions of stubbing out his cigarette, which was only half-smoked. But then, abruptly, he raised his eyes and looked at me.

"Here, you!"

Instead of passing on with downcast eyes as I should have done, I stood there rooted to the spot like a frightened rabbit.

"You—come over here!"

"Me?"

Blushing at what I felt was the childish tone of my reply, I stepped through the bamboo grass and presented myself before them.

"Here—come and sit down."

"Yessir."

By now he had put another cigarette in his mouth and lit it. Then, once I was seated, he held out the pack to me. Alarmed, I pushed it away.

"Go on—try one. They're better than candy."

"But I . . ."

He lit another cigarette himself and forced me to take it.

"It'll go out if you don't smoke it."

I took a puff. A smell like that of the marsh a while ago mingled with the fragrance of burning leaves, and I had a momentary vision of some great tropical tree all in flames. . . .

I was seized with a violent fit of coughing. The older boys looked at each other and laughed gleefully. The tears that unexpectedly came into my eyes gave me a feeling of happiness oddly in accord with their delighted laughter. Why? With an embarrassed grin I sprawled out on the ground, face up. The stiff blades of the grass pricked at my back through the thinnish material of my school uniform. Lifting my first cigarette high in the air, my eyes half-closed, I gazed avidly at the smoke trailing into the shadowy blue of the afternoon sky. It rose gracefully; it lingered, wavered in an almost imperceptible cloud; like a dream just before waking, it took shape only, ineffectually, to dissolve again.

The drugged passage of time was broken by a gentle, kindly

sounding voice that murmured in my ear: "What's your name, kid?"

It was the one who had given me the cigarette. I could scarcely believe my ears: here, it seemed, was the voice I'd been waiting for ever since I could remember.

"Nagasaki."

"First grade?"

"Yes."

"What club?"

"I haven't yet ..."

"Which are you going to join, then?"

I hesitated. Eventually, sheer indifference got the better of the false reply that would have ingratiated me with him.

"The literature club."

"Literature! ...." The cry, almost of pain, overlapped with my answer. "You can't do that! It's a home for consumptives. You ought to know better than that!"

But I merely gazed at his expression of stupefaction with an equivocal little smile. It gave me the courage to get up. On my feet, I looked at my watch, frowning and peering at it as though I was shortsighted.

"I've got some business to see to...."

At this, the one who'd been lying on the ground sat up.

"Hey—you're not going off to blab about us, are you?"

"Don't worry," I said, in the businesslike tone of a hospital nurse. "I'm going to the shop that sells fountain pens.... Well—goodbye, then."

As I set off down the rounded slope I heard a distant voice saying behind me, "He's gone off in a huff." It was the cheerful, matter-of-fact tone of the boy who'd given me the cigarette.

For some reason, I felt an urge to look back toward that youthful voice. But just then a brief, breathtaking glimpse of something crimson behind a clump of trees a short way ahead distracted me. Even so, my mind must have been elsewhere, for before I realized it I'd gone right past that beautiful splash of red. I turned around. It was a young cherry tree, its foliage colored right down to its lower branches. The sunlight filtering from the trees above shone through the clear crimson, emphasizing its artificial, fragile beauty. Even the all-pervading autumn light seemed to be holding its breath; it was as though everything was seen through polished amber.

On my return home, remorse began to gnaw at me: or rather, a guilty fear. I felt as though there was still a cigarette down there between my fingers. When I settled in my chair to start studying, another, different uneasiness began to prey on me. I suddenly felt sure that however much I scrubbed at the smell of nicotine on my fingers, it wouldn't go away but would linger on, like the smell of broth on the man who had his fingers cut off in the *Arabian Nights*. Even if I swathed my hands in bandages, covered them with gloves so that I thought everything was hidden, people around me on the streetcar to school would sniff out the truth and stare at me as if I were a criminal. I imagined my own wretchedness when I finally realized that the smell, to be thus impossible to conceal, must have penetrated right inside me.

At dinner that evening, I was unable to look my father in the eye. Even my grandmother's usual mealtime warnings—"Kei, you're spilling your soup!"—made me start guiltily. When Grandmother was a girl, or so I'd been told, she'd been so canny that she could sense immediately if, say, a maid had been pilfering things. Almost certainly she knew I'd been smoking. The idea was too frightening for me to bear alone, so after the meal I went to her room with the idea of asking her not to betray me to my father. But she greeted this unusual visit with cries of surprise and proceeded to ply me with tea and cakes, leaving me no chance to speak. I ended up being taught the famous passage from the Noh play *Hashi-Benkei* that begins: "The color of the waves at dusk / Foretells perhaps a storm by night. . . ."

My uneasy suspicion of her only deepened all the more.

At school the next day, I felt that I was seeing everything with different eyes. What could have brought about this change? The only real possibility I could think of was the cigarette. The contempt I usually felt for those classmates of mine, the sporty types who associated with the older boys and talked all the time about girls, had been nothing, I now realized, but sour grapes, since my lack of interest in them seemed to be gradually turning into a desire to compete. I resolved that from now on, if they said to me, "You can swank all you like about those rhymes of yours, Nagasaki," (everything was "rhymes" to them, from haiku to modern verse), "but I bet you've never smoked," I would no longer stand in embarrassed silence, but would reply, to their discomfort: "Of course I have—what's so special about *that*?"

Why was it, even so, that the guilty dread of the night before, far from clashing with this new audacity, seemed subtly to reinforce it? In the scramble for seats in the science class (not at the front, but right at the back) I didn't, as usual, take my time and go to sit in whatever seat was vacant. Instead, I was right on the heels of the first boy who dashed off ahead of all the others after morning assembly.

As a result, the boy who usually sat in the second-best place (which meant a place where you could doze without being seen) found me sitting there already.

"Hey, Nagasaki—," he demanded resentfully, "what're you up to? Don't you know this is the worst place for getting picked on? You must've done your homework even better than usual!"

"Go and stuff yourself, Gas Mask," I replied, deliberately using the nickname given him by the older boys; and he ended up sitting down angrily in the foremost row, right in front of the teacher, where—much to everyone's delight—he was called on to answer a whole string of questions.

During the lunch break, I actually joined in playing basketball, a thing I'd never once done before. I was so hopeless, though, that I ended up as a reserve, and began to feel I was selling myself for friendship. Leaving the others at their game, I strolled over to the flower beds at the back of the school buildings.

Most of the flowers were over by now; all that remained was a mass of chrysanthemums, and even these generally had leaves tinged a pale yellow, so that the still-blooming flowers stood out with an almost artificial vividness. There was one extraordinarily elaborate bloom at which I stared and stared, till the mass of narrow yellow petals with their delicate vertical stripes seemed to swell up to ridiculous proportions, and my whole field of vision was occupied by one giant chrysanthemum. The air was full of the lethargic midday song of insects. I stood, head bent, for so long that when I straightened up my brain swam a little, and I felt ashamed at having let myself get absorbed in just one flower. Normally, even during those walks through the woods of which I was so fond, I never became so preoccupied with one particular thing. And I detected, unmistakably, a kind of bashfulness that I didn't have when gazing at some larger scene.

I was on my way back to the school buildings, hurrying slightly, when I saw again, below me in the distance, the ponds gleaming in the peaceful autumn sun. I recalled the regular, incisive sound of the axe, and the arrows of light darting from the glittering edge of the clouds—and, along with them, that cheerful,

118

matter-of-fact voice. As I did so, I felt my chest gripped by a violent yet somehow numbingly peaceful emotion. Whether it was associated with the cheerful voice I couldn't tell, but it was almost indistinguishable from the sense of achieved identity, identity with a well-remembered stillness flowing from some previous existence, that had overcome me by the pond as I looked up at the light escaping through the clouds.

Even so, as the days went by I gradually took leave of that alien brashness and, with it, the remorse and fear. The scent of the cigarette alone stayed with me, unforgettable. Far from fading with familiarity, it troubled me with an even greater sense of reality than before. To be near my father when he was smoking a cigar was to experience—the reverse side of a certain pleasure—an alarming nausea.

Quite swiftly, my tastes were turning away from what was peaceful and placid toward the noisy and meretricious things that I'd always so despised. One night, on the way back from a visit with my parents and grandmother to a fashionable restaurant in the heart of town, they decided for the sake of my grandmother, who couldn't walk very much, to have the cab make a slight detour so that we could see the bright lights of a late autumn evening. The adults were sitting in the back, with me on the extra seat staring at the outside scene, which, familiar though it was, had never seemed so attractive as it did that night. The clusters of crudely winking neon signs, the garishly bright shop windows, were none of them beautiful seen individually, yet taken together, so that they acquired an odd integrity, they were like a huge, ghostly firework that had not died out but remained suspended in the night sky, delicately shimmering there for all eternity.

I remembered a phrase, "the ephemeral city," that I had come across in a book at school. Yes, ephemeral was the right word, I decided: before anyone realized it—even the people living there—the streets would have changed into something different. Today's streets were not tomorrow's, nor were tomorrow's those of the day after.... Suddenly, I noticed a beautiful building shaped like a steamship. Unlike the other buildings with their gaudy lights, this was a pure white structure floating in a dim, smoky, unrelieved blue. Then, as I watched, a silent shadow rose up and the building rocked exactly as though it were floating on water. In astonishment I pressed my face still closer to the window.

"You've taken quite a fancy to the Ginza, haven't you!" said my mother with a loud laugh, breaking the silence.

My grandmother laughed too and added something about it being best not to get *too* fond of it. My father chuckled without removing the cigar from his mouth. Making no reply, I stiffened slightly, and ostentatiously went on gazing at the chain of lights beyond the window. At that moment, the car swung sharply around in a great curve to the right.

The streets here, unexpectedly, were dimly lit. I cast a pleading look, pregnant with a sense of loss, over the dark rooftops. A diadem of lights crowning the top of one large building was still visible. Then, like a vanishing moon, it too sank below the roofs, and the rest was a sky blurred with a light like the first glow of dawn.

Winter was drawing near when, one day after school, having something to look up for my homework, I got one of the committee members to let me have the key to the literary club's room, and let myself into its long-undusted interior. Finding a detailed dictionary of literature in one of the bookcases, I rested the heavy volume on my knees as I read. Then, deciding it was too much trouble to put it away again, I let my eyes wander from the original entry, and before I realized it the already uncertain sunlight had faded to a dim underwater glow.

Hastily putting the book away, I left the room. Outside, I encountered a medley of boisterous laughter and heavy footsteps, and a group of people came charging around the corner of the corridor. I couldn't make them out clearly against the light, but I recognized them as older boys, members of the rugby club. I bowed. As I did so, one of them, almost colliding with me, clapped me heartily on the shoulder and said,

"It's Nagasaki, isn't it?"

There was no mistaking the brisk, youthful voice. I looked up at him, almost tearful with emotion.

"Yes, that's right."

This caused an uproar. "Hey—the fancy boy!" "This should be fun!" "Not *another* one, Imura?"

"Here, Nagasaki—," said Imura, deliberately ignoring the banter, "come along to our place," and putting an arm around my shoulders he dragged me off in the direction of the rugby club's room. This only added to their excitement, and we were more or less propelled along to the room by force.

It was so cluttered you could hardly get a foot inside the door. But the first thing that struck you was the smell: strong, complex—perhaps "disturbing" would describe it best. It was different from the smell of the judo club: more melancholy, to the point of despair; intense, yet with something impermanent about it; precisely the same as the smell that had bothered me so persistently after I'd had the cigarette—less the real smell of a cigarette than an imagined one.

I was told to sit in a ramshackle chair beside a ramshackle table. Imura sat down next to me. His chair, which looked much sturdier than mine, creaked in a satisfying way whenever he stirred, giving a sense of solidity that I responded to directly.

121

Cold though it was, he was still in his rugger clothes, with bare knees, and the sweat hadn't yet dried on his face and chest.

At first, the others went on making remarks about me and Imura, who listened to their chaffing with every sign of interest, puffing at a cigarette all the while. For all the attention they paid me personally, I might not have been there. There was one other boy smoking: that was all. Casting an eye from time to time at Imura's sturdy arms, I did my best to behave in a childish manner. I even caught myself, with a slight sense of horror, laughing in a surprisingly loud voice.

As soon as the rest had more or less tired of teasing him, Imura, in his familiar brisk voice, launched into a commentary on the day's rugby practice. The faces around him regained their boyish earnestness. I listened to the voice with eyes closed. Opening them, I saw the cigarette getting shorter between his thick fingers. Suddenly, I had a choking sensation.

"Imura—" As I spoke up, they turned their eyes on me in unison. Desperately, I went on:

"May I have a cigarette, please?"

The older boys burst out laughing. Most of them had never even smoked themselves.

"Wow!" "What a cool little man!" "Just what you'd expect of Imura's little pal!"

I had the fleeting impression that the dark curve of Imura's brow had contracted slightly. Nevertheless, he deftly extracted a cigarette from his case.

"Are you sure you want it?" he said, handing it over.

I'm certain that the reply I'd hoped for was something quite different, though it would have been hard to put in words. I'd staked everything on the one, correct answer. Even more crucial, perhaps, was the inexplicable, desperate urge to let his reply somehow determine, once and for all, the way I lived my life from that point on. But I had lost the will even to consider such questions; I gazed at Imura vacantly, like a sheep that, having no words, can only communicate its grief by staring into its master's eyes.

Still, it was too late not to smoke. In the event, I coughed and wheezed without stopping. Blinking through my tears, I smoked on in the face of imminent nausea. A cold grip constricted the rear half of my brain, the room seen through my tears had an unnatural glitter, the laughing faces of the other boys were grotesque figures in a Goya etching. But their laughter was no longer unconstrained; as the ripples died down, other, more painful feelings were clearly revealed lurking underneath, threatening them. The group was becoming more subdued, preparing to view me with different eyes. For the first time, I stared through my tears at Imura, sitting by my side.

He was deliberately avoiding looking at me. He perched on the edge of his chair, elbows on the table, in a precarious-looking posture. An artificial smile on his face, he was gazing at a fixed spot on the table. Taking in the sight, I experienced a sudden pang of joy: he was upset. Was that why I was glad, though? Or was it because of the strange sense of fellowship I'd briefly known only to have it, painfully and paradoxically, vanish just as soon?

Suddenly Imura turned, the smile still frozen on his face. With a patent effort to seem casual, his hand stretched out, and before I realized what was happening he'd removed the half-smoked cigarette from my fingers.

"That's enough, now. Don't overdo it."

With his own strong fingers, he crushed it against the nicked edge of the table.

"It'll be dark soon. Shouldn't you be getting home?"

Seeing me stand up, the others chimed in:

"Can you get back by yourself?" "Say, Imura—why don't you go with him?"

But they obviously only wanted to please Imura. Bowing in quite the wrong direction, I left the room. As I walked along the corridor beneath the dim electric bulbs, the way home felt to me, for the first time, like a long journey stretching ahead.

Sleepless in bed that night, I thought things over to the utmost extent possible for someone of my age. What had happened to my pride? Hadn't I stubbornly resolved that I wouldn't be anything other than myself? It was as though things that I'd formerly seen as vaguely ugly had, in an instant, been transformed into beauty. Never before had I resented so strongly the fact that I was only a child. . . .

In the late hours of that night, as I remember it, there was a fire somewhere in the distance. I was still lying sleepless when the sound of the fire engine close at hand had me up and rushing to open the shutters. But the blaze was far off on the other side of town. The clamor of the fire engine's bell was still audible, but the distant view of the fire with its red blobs drifting gracefully up into the sky was oddly silent.

Steadily the flames gathered, renewed their force. The sight abruptly recalled me to sleepiness and, casually closing the shutters, I went back to bed and promptly fell asleep.

And yet the memory is unreliable in the extreme. For all I know, the whole scene of the fire may have been something that came to me in a dream that night.

MARTYRDOM

A diminutive Demon King ruled over the dormitory. The school in question was a place where large numbers of sons of the aristocracy were put through their paces. Equipped by the age of thirteen or fourteen with a coldness of heart and an arrogance of spirit worthy of many a grown-up, they were placed in this dormitory in their first year at middle school in order to experience communal life; this was one of the traditions of the spartan education devised several decades earlier by the principal of the school, General Ogi. The members of any one year had all been to the same primary school, so that their training in mischief had taken thorough effect in the six years before entering the dormitory, and facilitated an astonishing degree of collaboration among them. A "graveyard" would be arranged in a corner of the classroom with a row of markers bearing the teachers' names; a trap would be set so that when an elderly, bald teacher came into the room a blackboard duster fell precisely onto his bald patch, coating it with white; on a winter morning, a lump of snow would be flung to stick on the ceiling, bright in the morning sun, so that it dripped steadily onto the teacher's platform; the matches in the teachers' room would be mysteriously transformed into things that spouted sparks like fireworks when struck; a dozen drawing pins would be introduced into the chair where the teacher sat, with their points just showing above the surface—these and a host of other schemes that seemed the work of unseen elves were all in fact carried out by two or three masterminds and a band of well-trained terrorists.

"Come on—let's see it! What's wrong with showing me anyway?"

The older boy who had turned up in the lunch break lounged astride the broken dormitory chair. He could sense the itching curiosity in himself that crawled vaguely, like soft incipient beard, right up to his ears, but in trying to conceal it from the other, his junior by a year, he was only making his face turn all the pinker. At the same time, it was necessary to sit in as slovenly a way as possible in order to show his independence of the rules.

"I'll show you, don't worry. But you'll have to wait another five minutes. What's up, K?—it's not like you to be so impatient."

The Demon King spoke boldly, gazing steadily at the older boy with mild, beautiful eyes. He was well developed for a mere fourteen, and looked in fact at least sixteen or seventeen. He owed his physique to something called the "Danish method" of child rearing—which involved among other things dangling the baby by one leg and kneading its soft, plump body like so much dough—and to the fact that he'd been brought up in a Western house with huge plate-glass windows standing on high ground in the Takanawa district of Tokyo, where breezes borne on bright wings from the distant sea would occasionally visit the lawn. Naked, he had the figure of a young man. During physical checkups, when the other boys were pale with dire embarrassment, he was a Daphnis surveying his nanny goats with cool, scornful eyes.

The dormitory was the farthest from the main school buildings, and the Demon King's room on the second floor looked out over the shimmering May woods covering the gentle slope of the school grounds. The long grass and undergrowth seemed almost tipsy as it swayed in the wind. It was morning, and the chirping of the birds in the woods was particularly noisy. Now and again, a pair of them would take off from the sea of young foliage and fly up like fish leaping from its surface, only to produce a sudden, furious twittering, turn a somersault, and sink down again between the waves of greenery.

When K, his senior, came to see him in his room bearing sandwiches and the like, it had been instantly apparent to the Demon King—young Hatakeyama—that the motive was a desire to see the book that everyone found so fascinating. To tease a senior pupil over something of this sort gave him a sweet sense of complicity, as though he too were being teased.

"Five minutes is up."

"No it isn't—it's only three minutes yet."

"It's five minutes!"

Quite suddenly, Hatakeyama gave him an almost girlish smile, the vulnerable smile of someone who had never yet had anyone be rude to him.

"Oh well, I suppose it can't be helped," he said. "I'll let you see it."

With his left hand thrust in his trouser pocket, as was his usual habit (in imitation of a cousin, a college student, whom he'd much admired for the way he let his shiny metal watchstrap show between the pocket and his sweater), he went lazily to open the bookcase. There, among the textbooks that he'd never once laid hands on after returning to the dorm, and the books his parents had bought for him—a grubby *Collected Boys' Tales*, the *Jungle Book*, and *Peter Pan* in paperback editions—there ought to have stood a volume with "*Plutarch's Lives*" inscribed in immature lettering on its spine. This book, whose red cover he had wrapped in uninviting brown paper and labeled with a title that he had memorized from a work of about the same thickness seen in the library, was constantly being passed from hand to hand, during classes and in recess alike. People would have been startled to find, on the page that should have portrayed a statue of Alexander the Great, an odd, complex sectional diagram in color.

"It's no use suddenly pretending you can't find it!" Gazing at the Demon King's rear view as he ferreted through the contents of the bookshelves, K was less concerned with the desire to see the book as such than with making sure, first, that he wasn't cheated by this formidable younger schoolmate, and then that he didn't put himself at a disadvantage by clumsy bullying.

"Somebody's stolen it!" shouted Hatakeyama, standing up. He'd been looking down as he searched, and his face was flushed, his eyes gleaming. Rushing to his desk, he frantically opened and closed each drawer in turn, talking to himself all the while:

"I made a point of getting everyone who came to borrow that book to sign for it. I mean, I couldn't have people taking my stuff out without my permission, could I? That book was the class's special secret. It meant a lot to everybody. I was particularly careful with it—I'd never have let anyone I didn't like read it. . . ."

"It's a bit late to get so angry about it, surely," said K with an assumed maturity, then, noticing the brutal glint in Hatakeyama's eye, suddenly shut up. More than anything, the look reminded him of a child about to kill a snake.

"I'm *sure* it's Watari," said his crony Komiyama, writing the name "Watari" twice in small letters on the blackboard and pointing to the bright-lit doorway through which the boy in question, by himself as usual, had just gone out into the school yard. Beyond the doorway a cloud was visible, smooth and glossy, floating in the sky beyond the spacious playground. Its shadow passed ponderously across the ground.

"Watari? Come off it! What does a kid like him understand about a book like that?"

"A lot—you wait and see! Haven't you ever heard of the quiet lecher? It's types with saintly expressions like him who're most interested in that kind of thing. Try barging in on him in his room tonight before supper, when all the rest have gone for exercise and there's nobody in the dorm. You'll see!"

Alone of their group, Watari had come to them from another primary school, and was thus a comparative outsider. There was something about him that kept others at a distance. Although he was particular about his clothes—he changed his shirt every day—he would go for weeks without cutting his nails, which were always an unhealthy black. His skin was a yellowish, lusterless white like a gardenia. His lips, in contrast, were so red that you wanted to rub them with your finger to see if he was wearing lipstick. Seen close to, it was an astonishingly beautiful face, though from a distance quite unprepossessing. He reminded you of an art object in which excessive care over detail has spoiled the effect of the whole; the details were correspondingly seductive in a perverse way.

He had begun to be bullied almost as soon as he appeared at the school. He gave the impression of looking disapprovingly on the tendency, common to all boys, to worship toughness as a way of making up for their awareness of the vulnerability peculiar to their age. If anything, Watari sought to preserve the vulnerability. The young man who seeks to be himself is respected by his fellows; the boy who tries to do the same is persecuted by other boys, it being a boy's business to become something else just as soon as he can.

Watari had the habit, whenever he was subjected to particularly vile treatment by his companions, of casting his eyes up at the clear blue sky. The habit was itself another source of mockery.

"Whenever he's picked on, he stares up at the sky as if he was Christ," said M, the most persistent of his tormentors. "And you know, when he does it, his nose tips back so you can see right up his nostrils. He keeps his nose so well blown, it's a pretty pink color round the edges inside. . . ."

Watari was, of course, banned from seeing *"Plutarch's Lives."*

The sun had set on all but the trees in the woods. The dark mass of foliage, minutely catching the lingering rays of the setting sun, trembled like the flame of a guttering candle. As he stealthily opened the door and went in, the first thing Hatakeyama saw was the wavering trees through the window directly ahead. The sight of Watari registered next; he was seated at his desk, gazing down with his head in his delicate white hands, intent on something. The open pages of the book and the hands stood out in white relief.

He turned around at the sound of footsteps. The next instant, his hands covered the book with an obstinate strength.

Moving swiftly and easily across the short space that separated them, Hatakeyama had seized him by the scruff of the neck almost before he realized it himself. Watari's large, expressionless eyes, wide open like a rabbit's, were suddenly close to his own face. He felt his knees pressing into the boy's belly, eliciting a strange sound from it as he sat on the chair; then he knocked aside the hands that tried to cling to him, and dealt a smart slap to his cheek. The flesh looked soft, as though it might stay permanently dented. For one moment, indeed, Watari's face seemed to tilt in the direction in which it had been struck, assuming an oddly placid, helpless expression. But then the cheek rapidly flooded with red and a thin, stealthy trickle of blood ran from the finely shaped nostrils. Seeing it, Hatakeyama felt a kind of pleasant nausea. Taking hold of the collar of Watari's blue shirt, he dragged him toward the bed, moving with unnecessarily large strides as though dancing. Watari let himself be dragged, limp as a puppet; curiously, he didn't seem to grasp the situation he was in, but gazed steadily at the evening sky over the woods with their lingering light. Or perhaps those big, helpless eyes simply let in the evening light quite passively, taking in the sky without seeing anything. The blood from his nose, though, cheerfully seemed to flaunt its glossy brightness as it dribbled down his mouth and over his chin.

"You thief!"

Dumping Watari on the bed, Hatakeyama climbed onto it himself and started trampling and kicking him. The bed creaked, sounding like ribs breaking. Watari had his eyes shut in terror. At times, he bared his over-regular teeth and gave a thin wail like a small sick bird. Hatakeyama thumped him in the side for a while, then, seeing that he had turned toward the wall and gone still, like a corpse, jumped down from the bed in one great leap. As a finishing touch, he remembered to thrust one guilty hand elegantly into the pocket of his narrow slacks and tilt himself slightly to one side. Then, whisking up *"Plutarch's Lives"* from the desk with his right hand, he tucked it stylishly under his arm and ran up the stairs to his second-floor room.

He had read the dubious book in question quite a few times. Each time, the first frenzied excitement seemed to fade a little. Recently in fact he had begun to get more pleasure, if anything, out of observing the powerful spell the book exerted over his friends as they read it for the first time. But now, reading it again himself after getting it back and roughing up Watari in the process, the original, wild excitement emerged as a still fiercer pleasure. He couldn't get through a single page at a time. Each appearance of one of those words of almost mystic power brought a myriad associations crowding, plunged him into an ever deeper intoxication. His breath grew shallower, his hand trembled, the bell for supper that happened just then to resound through the dormitory almost made him panic: how could he appear before the others in this state? He had entirely forgotten Watari.

That night, a dream woke Hatakeyama from a troubled sleep. The dream had led him to the lairs of various illnesses that he had suffered from in childhood. In actual fact, few children could have been healthier than he: the only illnesses he'd succumbed to were of the order of whooping cough, measles, and intestinal catarrh. Nevertheless, the diseases in his dream were all acquainted with him, and greeted him accordingly. Whenever one of them approached him, there was a disagreeable smell; if he tried to shove it away, "disease" transferred itself stickily to his hand like oil paint. One disease was even tickling his throat with its finger. . . .

When he awoke, he found himself staring, wide-eyed like a rabbit, in just the way that Watari had done earlier that day. And there, floating above the covers, was Watari's startled face, a mirror of his own. As their eyes met, the face rose slowly into the air.

Hatakeyama let out a high-pitched yell. At least, he thought he did: in fact his voice rose only as far as his throat.

Something was pressing down steadily, with cold hands, on his throat; yet the pressure was slight enough to be half pleasant. Deciding that it was a continuation of his dream after all, he extracted a hand unhurriedly from the bedclothes and stroked himself experimentally around the neck. It appeared that something like a cloth sash, about two inches wide, had been wrapped snugly around it.

He had the courage and good sense to fling it off without further ado. He sat up in bed, looking much older than he was, more like a young man of twenty. A chain of ivory clouds, lit up by the moon, was passing across the window outside, so that he was silhouetted against it like the statue of some god of old.

The thing that crouched like a dog at the foot of the bed had a white, human face turned resolutely toward him. It seemed to be breathing heavily, for the face as a whole appeared to swell and shrink; the eyes alone were still, overflowing with a shining light as they gazed, full of hostility (or was it longing?), at Hatakeyama's shadowed features.

"Watari. You came to get even, didn't you?"

Watari said nothing, the lips that were like a rose in the dark night quivering painfully. Finally, he said as though in a dream:

"I'm sorry."

"You wanted to kill me, I suppose."

"I'm sorry." He made no attempt to run away, simply repeating the same phrase.

Without warning, Hatakeyama flew at him and, propelled by the bedsprings, carried him face down onto the floor. There, kneeling astride him, he subjected him to a full twenty minutes' violence. "I'm going to make sure you feel ashamed in front of everyone in the bath!" he promised, then splashed his bare buttocks with blue-black ink; prodded them with the points of a pair of compasses to see their reaction; reared up, hauling the boy up by the ears as he did so. . . . He was brilliantly methodical, as though everything had been thought out in advance. There was no chance, even, for Watari to look up at the sky this time. He

135

lay still, his cheek pressed against a join in the linoleum.

Two boys were allotted to each room in the dormitory, but Hatakeyama's roommate was home on sick leave. So long as he was careful not to be overheard downstairs, Hatakeyama could do as he wished.

Eventually, both of them began to tire. Before they realized it they were dozing, sprawled on the floor; Watari had even forgotten to cover his pale behind.

Their nap lasted no more than a moment. Hatakeyama awoke first. Pillowing his chin on clasped hands, he gazed at the moonlit window. All that was visible from the floor where he lay was the sky. The moon was below the frame of the window, but two or three clouds could be seen in the sky's fullness of limpid light. The scene had the impersonal clarity, precision, and fineness of detail of a scene reflected in the polished surface of a piece of machinery. The clouds seemed stationed as immovably as some majestic man-made edifice.

An odd desire awoke in Hatakeyama, taking him by surprise. It wasn't so much a break with the mood of tranquillity as a natural transition from it, and in a strange way it was linked with the terrifying sensation of the cord around his neck that he'd experienced a while before. This, he thought, is the fellow who tried to kill me. And suddenly a peculiar sense of both superiority and inferiority, a nagging humiliation at not in fact having been killed, made it impossible for him to stay still.

"You asleep?" he said.

"No," said Watari. As he replied, his eyes turned to look straight at Hatakeyama. He began to stretch out his thin right arm, then drew it in again and pressed it to his side, saying,

"It hurts here."

"Really? Does it *really* hurt?"

Hatakeyama rolled over twice. It brought him a little too

close, so that he was lying half on top of Watari. Just as this happened, the latter gave a faint little chuckle, a sound—like the cry of a shellfish—he had never heard before. The Demon King sought out the sound, then pressed his whole face against Watari's lips and the soft down around them.

There was something going on between Hatakeyama and Watari: their classmates passed on the rumor in hushed voices. The scandal possessed a mysterious power; thanks to it, Hatakeyama became increasingly influential, and even Watari was taken into their circle. The process was similar to that whereby a woman so far generally ignored suddenly acquires value in everyone's eyes if the dandy of the group takes a fancy to her. And it was totally unclear how Hatakeyama himself responded to this general reaction.

Before long, it was felt that his authority as Demon King required some kind of strict legal system. They would draft the necessary laws during their English and spelling lessons. The criminal code, for example, must be an arbitrary one, based on the principle of intimidation. A strong urge to self-regulation had awoken in the boys. One morning in the dormitory, the gang insisted that their leader pick out someone for them to punish. They were sitting in their chairs in a variety of bizarre postures; some were not so much seated in them as clinging to them. One first-grader had turned his chair upside down and was sitting holding on to two projecting legs.

"Hatakeyama—you've got to name somebody. You name him, and the rest of us'll deal with him. Isn't there anyone who's been getting above himself lately?"

"No, no one." He spoke in a surly voice, his mature-looking back turned to them.

"You sure? Then we'll choose the person ourselves."

"Wait a minute! What I said wasn't true. Listen: I'll name someone. But I won't say why."

They waited breathlessly; there wasn't one of them who didn't want to hear his own name mentioned.

"Where's Watari?"

"Watari?—he went off somewhere just now."

"OK, it's him. He's been getting uppish. If we don't put a stop to it, he'll get completely out of hand."

This was pure imitation of fifth-grader talk. Even so, having got it out, Hatakeyama looked cheerfully relieved, like someone remembering something till then forgotten. It provoked a happy clamor among the others:

"Let's fix the time—the lunch break!"

"And the place—by Chiarai Pond."

"I'll take my jackknife."

"And I'll bring a rope. If he struggles we can tie him up."

On a pond already green with slime the surrounding trees spread an even reflection of lush young foliage, so that anyone who walked beside it was steeped in its green light. They were all privately enjoying the important sound of their own feet tramping through the bamboo grass, and the party with Hatakeyama and Watari at its center exchanged no words. Watari showed no sign of fear as he walked, a fact that had a disturbing effect on his classmates, as though they were watching a very sick man, supposedly on his last legs, suddenly striding along. From time to time, he glanced up at the sky visible through the new leaves of the treetops. But the others were all too sunk in their own thoughts for anyone to remark on his behavior. Hatakeyama walked with long strides, head bent, left hand in pocket. He avoided looking at Watari.

Halting, Hatakeyama raised both arms in their rolled-up sleeves above his head:

"Stop! Quiet!"

An elderly gardener was pushing a wheelbarrow along the path above them toward the flower beds.

"Well, well—up to some mischief, I suppose," he said, seeing them.

"Dirty old scrounger!" someone replied. It was rumored that the old man lived off free dormitory leftovers.

"He's gone." M gave a signal with his eyes.

"Right. Here, Watari—"

For the first time, Hatakeyama looked straight into his eyes. Both Watari and his companions had unusually grave expressions.

"You've been getting too big for your boots."

No more was said: the sentence was passed; but nothing was done to carry it out. The judge stood with bare arms folded, slowly stroking them with his fingertips.... At that moment, Watari seemed to see his chance. Quite suddenly, he lunged toward Hatakeyama as though about to cling to him. Behind the latter lay the pond. As he braced his legs, stones and soil rolled down into it with a faint splashing. That was the only sound; to those around them, the two seemed locked in an embrace, silently consoling each other. But in steadying himself to avoid falling backward, Hatakeyama had exposed his arms to an attack already planned. Watari's teeth—regular and sharp as a girl's, or perhaps a cat's—sank into his young flesh. Blood oozed out along the line between teeth and skin, yet biter and bitten remained still. Hatakeyama didn't even groan.

A slight movement separated them. Wiping his lips, more crimson than ever with the blood, Watari stood still, his eyes

139

fixed on Hatakeyama's wound. A second or two before the members of the group had grasped what had happened, Watari had started running. But his pursuers were six tough boys. He lost his footing on the clay by the pond. He resisted, so that his blue shirt tore to give a glimpse of one shoulder, almost pathologically white. The boy with the rope tied his hands behind his back. His trousers, soiled by the red clay, were an oddly bright, shiny color.

Hatakeyama had made no move to chase him. His left hand was thrust casually into his pocket, with no care for his wound. The blood dripped down steadily, making a red rim around the glass of his wristwatch, then seeping from his fingertips into the bottom of his pocket. He felt no pain, aware only of something that hardly seemed like blood, something warm and familiar and intensely personal, caressing the surface of his skin as it went. But he had made up his mind on one thing: in his friends' faces when they brought Watari back, he would see nothing but an embodiment of his own decision, inviting him to proceed.

After that, he didn't look at Watari but gazed steadily at the long rope to which he was tied, with the slack wound round and round him and its end held in the hand of one of his classmates.

"Let's go somewhere quiet," he said. "The little wood behind the pigeon lofts."

Prodded, Watari began walking. As they filed along the red clay path, he staggered again and fell to his knees. With a coarse "heave-ho," they yanked him to his feet. His shoulder stood out so white in the light reflected from the foliage that it was as though the bone was sticking out of the rent in his blue shirt.

All the time as Watari walked, the incorrigible M hung about him, tickling him under the arms, pinching his backside, roaring with laughter because the boy, he said, had looked up at the sky. What if he had known that only two things in the whole world were visible to Watari's eyes: the blue sky—the eye of God, forever striking down into men's eyes through the green leaves of the treetops—and the precious blood spilled on his own account down here on earth, the lifeblood staining Hatakeyama's arm? His gaze went continually from one to the other of these two things. Hatakeyama was looking straight ahead, walking with a confident step more adult than any adult's. On his left arm, just in front of Watari, the blood was slowly drying, showing up a bright purple whenever it passed through the sun's rays.

The grove behind the pigeon lofts was a sunny patch of widely spaced trees, little frequented, where the pigeons often came to pass the time. An undistinguished collection of smallish deciduous trees, it had, at its very center, one great pine with gently outstretched branches on which the birds were fond of lining up to coo at one another. The rays of the afternoon sun picked out the trunk of the pine in a bright, pure light so that the resin flowing from it looked like veins of agate.

Hatakeyama came to a halt and said to the boy holding the rope:

"All right—this'll do. Take the rope off Watari. But don't let him get away. Throw the thing up like a lasso and put it over that big branch on the pine tree."

The rich jest of this sent the others into ecstasies. Watari was being held down by two of them. The remaining four danced like little demons on the grass as they helped hitch up the rope. One end of it was tied in a loop. Then one of the boys mounted a handy tree stump, poked his head through the noose, and stuck out his tongue.

"That's no good—it'll have to be higher."

The boy who'd stuck his tongue out was the shortest of them all. Watari would need at least another two or three inches.

They were all scared, scared by the occasional, shadowy suggestion that their prank might possibly be in earnest. As they led Watari, pale and trembling slightly, to the waiting noose, one waggish youth delivered a funeral address. All the while, Watari continued to gaze up at the sky with his idiotically wide-open eyes.

Abruptly, Hatakeyama raised a hand by way of a signal. His eyes were shut tight.

The rope went up.

Startled by the sudden beating of many pigeons' wings and by the glow on Watari's beautiful face, astonishingly high above them, they fled the grove, each in a different direction, unable to bear the thought of staying at the scene of such dire murder.

They ran at a lively pace, each boyish breast still swelling with the pride of having killed someone.

A full thirty minutes later, they reentered the wood as though by agreement and, huddling together, gazed up fearfully at the branch of the great pine.

The rope was dangling free, the hanged corpse nowhere to be seen.

ACT
OF
WORSHIP

1

When first commanded by Professor Fujimiya to accompany him on a pilgrimage to the Kumano shrines, Tsuneko was thoroughly startled.

It was meant, apparently, as a way of thanking her for looking after his personal needs for the past ten years. A widow of forty-five with no one of her own, she had first come to him for private tuition in writing Japanese verse; then, finding that the old woman who kept house for him had just, most inconveniently, died, she had begun to look after him herself. In all those ten years, though, there had not been the least hint of anything erotic between them.

She had never been beautiful, and lacked all feminine appeal. Utterly undistinguished by nature, self-effacing in everything, she was constitutionally incapable of making demands on other people. Even her marriage to a man who had died after two years had been no love match, but one imposed on her by relatives. It was odd that such a woman should have taken to writing poetry, but it was precisely this personality of hers, it seemed, together with her lack of any special gifts, that had made the Professor decide to take her into his house.

Even so, a more basic reason behind the move was Tsuneko's own need to look up to someone; and for this there was no worthier object than Professor Fujimiya.

The Professor, who held the chair of Japanese literature at Seimei University, was a Doctor of Letters and himself well known as a poet. His studies of the "Kokin mysteries," a secret literary tradition based on the *Kokinshu* anthology of verse, were noted for elucidating the process—a subtle fusion of aristocratic and popular culture—whereby the debased tradition of the courtly literature of the Heian period, while increasingly lapsing into empty form, became involved with popular religious beliefs and grew increasingly mystic in character until finally, in the Tokugawa period, it produced a peculiar cult in which Shinto, Buddhist, and Confucian theories were oddly mingled. During the past ten years these studies had been succeeded by others involving another secret tradition derived from the *Tale of Genji*. The result was that the Professor's lectures on Heian literature tended to stray from their proper path and to acquire the medieval flavor of these traditions.

Alongside the devotion to scientific proof and methodicalness that characterized his work, it was the mystic that held the greatest fascination for him: he was, above all, a poet. His approach to the celebrated *Mystery of the Three Birds*, a key work in one of the traditions, was a case in point. He took as his subject the three birds of the title, *inaosedori*, *momochidori*, and *yobukodori*—which are of course imaginary birds not to be found in any zoo, mystic symbols of the three great principles of the universe—and drew a parallel with the flowers in Zeami's *Kadensho*. His ideas were embodied in his own *Flowers and Birds*, a work whose prose-poem beauty had given it a wide readership.

Around him had gathered a swarm of followers to whom he was a god; each of them eyed the others jealously lest a rival should usurp his favor, and it was no easy matter for him to observe a proper fairness among them.

All this might suggest that the Professor, at both the social and individual levels, cut a rather dazzling figure. Yet to those who associated with him personally no one could have been more solitary and outlandish.

He was, for one thing, unprepossessing in the extreme. A childhood injury had left him with a walleye and an accompanying sense of inferiority that accounted in part for the gloom and inwardness of his personality. There were times, it's true, when he would joke with those close to him—would demonstrate, even, the hectic liveliness of a sickly child at play—yet nothing succeeded in obliterating the air of introspection, or in transcending the suggestion of excessive self-awareness, like wings unsuitably large for the body, in a man who was thoroughly acquainted with his own disposition and accepted the limitations it imposed.

The Professor had a peculiar soprano voice which in moments of great intensity would acquire an almost metallic ring. Even those in closest attendance on him could never tell when he might fly into a rage. From time to time, during one of his lectures, a student would be ordered without explanation to leave the room. The reason, on closer inquiry, might prove to be that the student in question had been wearing a bright red sweater that day, or that he'd been scratching his head with a pencil and scattering dandruff.

Yet even now, at the age of sixty, the Professor retained a gentler, weaker, and more childlike side to his character. Conscious of it, he was always afraid that it might lose him the respect of others, and was correspondingly insistent that his students should observe the proprieties. Even so, students from other faculties who had no interest whatever in his academic achievements had dubbed him "Dr. Weirdo."

The spectacle of the Professor crossing the cheerful modern campus of Seimei University with a bunch of his disciples in tow was so eye-catching that it had become one of the famous local sights. Wearing glasses tinted a pale mauve, clad in a badly fitting, old-fashioned suit, he walked with the feeble sway of a willow tree in the wind. His shoulders sloped steeply and his trousers were baggy, ill contrasting with hair that was dyed black and slicked down to an unnatural neatness. The students who walked behind him bearing his briefcase wore, as was only to be expected of such a resolutely anachronistic crew, the black uniforms with stiff white collars that everyone else at the university shunned; it gave them the air of a suite of ill-omened ravens. As in the sickroom of someone gravely ill, they were not permitted to speak in loud or over-lively voices. Such conversation as took place was carried out in whispers, so that people watching from a distance would remark with amusement: "There goes the funeral again!"

Not that levity was entirely absent. For instance, as they passed close to some students playing American football, one of the Professor's followers might say,

"Miyazaka composed a piece of doggerel the other day, sir:

See, the Merikens
At their muddy *kemari*—
The days are drawing out,"

to which the Professor would reply in fine good humor:

"I won't have that! It's not so much the quality of the verse I object to, but he should pay me a royalty for use of the phrase. I refuse to comment on the poem till he's done so!"

This would be one of the master's and disciples' happier moments. "Muddy *kemari*" was a phrase the Professor had invented in a recent verse satirizing football—*kemari* being the slow, dignified game played at the ancient imperial court—and the point of the joke was that the student had misappropriated his new coinage. This kind of humor had a subtly fawning air

148

reminiscent of puppies playing with one eye on their watchful parent. But no one, in practice, qualified as a student of the Professor's unless he found such things genuinely funny.

At times like this a light murmur of laughter, like rising dust in spring, would float up from the flock of ravens; the Professor himself rarely laughed out loud. Then, almost immediately, the mirth would die down again. To a distant observer, the impression would be of some weird ritual game in which a gloomily reverent group bound by secret rites had momentarily compromised the rules governing the expression of the emotions, thereby tightening still further the bonds, so incomprehensible to others, that held it together.

Occasionally, the sorrow and loneliness that lay so heavy in the Professor's heart would find an outlet in his poetry, but at normal times they were only to be glimpsed faintly—through glass, as it were, as one glimpses strange fish lurking behind rocks in an aquarium. There was no indication of what it was that confined the Professor within this personal grief; nor did those who pressed the question maintain any lasting acquaintance with him. Now and again, he would favor the innermost circle of his followers with a disquisition on "the canker, melancholy," that afflicted him:

"According to Robert Burton's classic theory, there are four types of humor in the human body—blood, phlegm, choler, and melancholy. The last-named, a cold, thick, black acidic fluid, is produced by the spleen, and its function (according to Burton) is to regulate the blood and bile, as well as to give nourishment to the bones. Among the things cited as causes of melancholia are the influence of spirits, demons, and the heavenly bodies. Where foodstuffs are concerned, beef in particular is said to encourage melancholy—and, as you may have observed, I am fond of beef. According to Burton, moreover, the scholar's is by its nature the most unstable of occupations; whoever seeks to become an outstanding scholar and to master the whole range of knowledge is destined eventually to lose health, wealth—life itself. He is, accordingly, particularly prone to melancholia. In short, it would be remarkable, fulfilling all the conditions as I do, if I were *not* possessed by the canker of melancholy."

His listeners, knowing that he only said such things when he was in a good humor, would be perplexed as to whether they should take this seriously or not.

Another of the Professor's prominent qualities was a tendency to jealousy. Though a confirmed friend of youth, he had once overheard a favorite student, one of those permitted to attend the special seminars that he held at his own house, relating in a loud voice how he had made a hit with the proprietress of a certain bar, and had promptly excommunicated the boy in question on the grounds of unsuitable conduct. He always insisted that these special study meetings at his own residence should be wrapped in an aura of youthful purity, an aura akin to that enveloping the sanctuary of a Shinto shrine and as such suited to these sessions aimed at evoking the divine spirit of poesy. The smell of hair oil, the odor of unwashed linen, were taboo; his one desire on such occasions was that the cavernous gloom of his best room should be filled with the breath of youth, light and fresh as the fragrance of newly planed cedar wood, and with the shining eyes and young voices of innocent enthusiasm.

Inexpert in attack yet doughty in strategic withdrawal, the Professor had, even in wartime, proved beyond reproach in preserving the integrity of learning. It was one reason for the fanatic following he attracted in the postwar years.

The sorrow already mentioned pervaded not just his verse but his studies, the expression on his face, his clothing—indeed, everything about him. Walking alone, he went with downcast eyes; if he chanced to find a puppy, say, that had strayed onto the campus, he would squat down and stay there for a while, stroking its head. Even a strange, dirty, sore-infested puppy would make him stop, though he was too fastidious to consider keeping one at home. The impression he gave at such times was of wanting to see his solitude reaffirmed, framed like a picture, of deliberately seeking opportunities to act out the loneliness again for his own benefit. As he painted this picture of droll self-pity, the Professor's unnaturally black hair would gleam provocatively in the spring sunlight, and the shadows of the silk trees in the campus would flow down over his sloping shoulders—till suddenly the dog, sensing something wrong, would wrinkle its nose, draw in its tail, and withdraw hastily with a growl. Clasped in the hand with which the Professor had been stroking it lay one of the cotton pads soaked in alcohol that he always carried on his person. All but dripping with pure alcohol, the pads were prepared for him every morning without fail by Tsuneko: white, flossy wads packed in a shining silver container and yielding at the lightest touch a damp, volatile chill like that of melting frost. . . .

This, then, was the man and scholar in attending whom Tsuneko had spent ten years of her life.

The Fujimiya residence where the Professor, a perennial bachelor, lived his celibate life had its own strict and fastidious routine. The territories in which a woman was and was not permitted to set foot were clearly demarcated. The foods the Professor liked were: beef; a certain kind of snapper; persimmons; and such vegetables as field peas, brussels sprouts, and broccoli.

His only recreation was the Kabuki, which he would attend either in the company of his followers or with former disciples, at the invitation of the latter. Tsuneko had never once received a command to accompany him. Occasionally, he would give her half a day off with a suggestion that she "go and see a moving picture," but he never even mentioned going to the theater.

There was no television in the house, only an ancient radio with poor reception.

The Fujimiya residence was an old, purely traditional structure standing in its own garden, one of those that had survived the war in Masago-cho, in the Hongo district of Tokyo. Although the Professor disliked Western-style rooms—not a single chair was allowed in the house—at mealtimes he preferred, exceptionally, Western food. The kitchen, where he never went himself and into which even the students were not allowed, had become Tsuneko's solitary citadel. It never occurred to him, on the other hand, to modernize its facilities, which consisted solely of two old-fashioned gas rings. It was Tsuneko's skill alone that, on occasion, produced under such conditions a meal for a dozen or more people, and that made both ends meet every month; nor did a single complaint about recent rises in prices ever reach the Professor's ears.

Every morning and evening without fail he took a bath, but, despite Tsuneko's years of service, no traditional intimacies such as washing his back for him were permitted. Even to approach the Professor during his ablutions was strictly forbidden; once she had laid out a change of clothes in the anteroom and informed him that all was ready, it was safer for her to retreat to as great a distance as possible. On one occasion during the early days of her employment, she had been summoned by a clap of hands from the bathroom and had made the mistake of responding almost instantaneously—"Did you call, sir?"—from outside the frosted glass door beyond which the Professor's dim form moved. She had been roundly scolded for her pains. For a woman servant to appear too soon after such a summons was, in the Professor's eyes, improper.

152

The Fujimiya residence afforded plenty of retreats where a person could, if he or she so wished, get out of the way, but rooms that contained books in any number were out of bounds to women. It was forbidden to clean such rooms, much less lay hands on the books themselves without permission.

Books had spread like mold, eating their way through each of the ten rooms in turn. Overflowing from the study, they encroached on the next room, converting it into a kind of lightless dungeon, then spread along the corridors, making it impossible to pass without edging sideways. The tidying and dusting of the books, too, was permitted only to members of his inner circle, who vied with each other for the privilege. Nor was anyone really qualified for membership until, as a result of frequently performing such tasks, he was instantly able, on being given the title of a volume published in, say, 1897, to remember on what shelf it was kept.

The students and other disciples who frequented the house were forbidden to talk to Tsuneko in too friendly a manner. Ever since the occasion when a student, seeing her so hard worked, had been moved to offer a helping hand, thus incurring the Professor's displeasure, Tsuneko had had the sense not to make herself conspicuous in any way, or to speak more than was strictly necessary.

The one thing in life that Tsuneko had to look forward to was the poetry meeting held regularly every month. On that day alone, she was allowed to take her place at the foot of the table, was treated as one of the Professor's followers, and received an exhaustive criticism of her own efforts at writing verse. On ordinary days, there was little to do in the house, and she welcomed the solitude as a chance to devote herself to improving her slow-developing skills as a poet.

This, too, was one reason why Tsuneko looked up to the Professor as though he were a god, or the sun itself. At times other than the poetry meeting, he would never say a word to her about poetry. It was precisely because this was the kind of master she had always served that the star of the poetry meetings shone with a special brilliance in her eyes.

So routine had the feeling of reverence become in the Fujimiya household that it was difficult to believe that such emotions could count for so little in the world at large. As a scholar of Japanese literature of no ordinary accomplishment, as a poet who wrote both modern verse and traditional *tanka*, the Professor, in Tsuneko's eyes, occupied a middle ground between heaven and earth. Sometimes, even, she saw herself as a shrine maiden in a sort of secret religious community centering around his person.

That the Professor and Tsuneko lived alone together was a matter of common knowledge; various rumors had gone the rounds concerning them, and some of the women who attended the poetry meetings had gone so far as to cast insulting glances in her direction. She became correspondingly reticent in her behavior, eschewing all makeup and striving after an ever greater sobriety of dress, thinking nothing of making herself look, in the process, ten years older than her age.

A glance at the mirror made it quite obvious that her looks were not of a kind to find favor with men.

The face was entirely devoid of sexual appeal. None of its features would ever stir a man to amorous thoughts. The nose was undistinguished to a fault, the eyes were too narrow, the teeth tended to protrude, the cheeks were hollow and the ears poorly fleshed, while her figure as a whole lacked any sort of fullness. For the Professor to be coupled in rumor with a woman like herself would do infinite harm to his reputation, let alone her own. In dress and behavior therefore she must, she decided, maintain the style of—at best—a maidservant, a style as ill matched as possible to the Professor's standing.

At the same time, since the latter disliked any suggestion of slovenliness, she must avoid any laxness in her appearance. She should be simple and modest, and contrive thereby to make it all the clearer to others that she was not attractive.

All this trouble she took out of a sincere desire in everything to serve the Professor, who on his side accepted the service without giving the sincerity a second thought. Yet never for a moment did it occur to her to hold this against him.

Fortunately, as the years went by and she passed the forty mark without losing any of her deferential manner toward him, the rumors finally began to dwindle. She was beginning to look more and more elderly—to resemble, even, the frankly old woman whose place she had taken ten years earlier.

The Professor's daily routine was as follows.

Invariably he awoke at six, without having to be roused. Before this, therefore, it was necessary to clean out the rooms without making any noise, and to get the bath hot.

On rising, he didn't show himself immediately but went straight to the bathroom via the library. After gargling and washing, he had a leisurely soak in the bath, set razor to his barely perceptible beard, carefully dyed his hair, and got dressed. The existence of a poem in which he likened himself satirically to Saito Sanemori, the aging warrior who dyed his hair black lest he be thought too old for battle, suggested that on one score at least he was sensitive to public scrutiny.

In the meantime, Tsuneko would have prepared the breakfast and laid out the morning papers.

Next, the Professor would proceed to the domestic shrine, where he paid his respects in correct Shinto style, then sat himself at the breakfast table and bade Tsuneko, with whom this was the first encounter, good morning. Very occasionally, without smiling, he would make some obscure remark such as "I had a good dream last night. Something pleasant may be going to happen today," but for the most part he was silent. Except when he was traveling, and irrespective of the season, this same pattern was followed every morning. He was said to have been sickly in his youth, but for the past ten years he had had no illness at all to speak of.

In this way, Tsuneko lived totally hidden in his shadow, effacing her own personality, given solely to reverence and service. During the early years, there had been relatives who urged her to remarry. By now, however, tired of her stubbornness, they had ceased even to make hints. In taking Tsuneko into his household the Professor had, undeniably, shown a remarkably good eye for character.

Even so, several times a year, Tsuneko would sense a doubt sprouting in her mind like a mushroom, and would stamp it out in alarm.

It would happen on days when she was left alone to look after the spacious house.

On these occasions, she would often, quite suddenly, be inspired to write poetry. Where the urge came from she had no idea: strangely enough, she found she was able to write verse without feeling either joy or sorrow. Yet her habitual turns of phrase—which persisted however often the Professor tried to correct them—were in practice excessively influenced by the master's own poetry, or rather by the sadness that pervaded it.

"These aren't your own feelings," the Professor had once declared with severe sarcasm in front of the others. "You're simply borrowing the container of someone else's sorrow and putting yourself into it. It's like going to someone else's house to take a bath."

And she honestly felt it was so herself; but then, if there was anyone on earth who could make her feel *real* sadness, it was the Professor—and he refused to do so. She could only believe that her mentor, while himself vulnerable to the flux of unspecified emotions, was deliberately avoiding imparting either joy or grief to her.

The fact remained, however, that she was often visited by an urge to write verse; it was what gave meaning to her life. Which meant, surely, that the inspiration must come from within herself. Yet however consciously she delved, she failed to find any corresponding emotion deep inside her. Once, with the idea that it might reveal the world of her subconscious, she'd even tried writing a few poems in an avant-garde style, and had been roundly rebuked for it.

She would be standing, perhaps, facing the garden in the rainy season, looking at the clump of reeds planted in the foreground, darkened now with the threat of showers, with the distant rumbling of a train and the roar of cars reaching her ears across the gloom of the day. It was at times like this that the desire to write occurred; but always something in her own mind, something about the opening line, got in the way. Should it be, say, "The dead one . . ."? No—that gave the inappropriate impression that she was still bothered by her husband's death, which in fact had long ceased to mean anything to her. "The distant one . . ."? That was equally unsuitable, in that it suggested longing for an absent lover, which was nonsense. The words in short didn't flow naturally, but came filtered through a kind of weir.

This sadness that strayed into her mind at the sight of objects in the natural scene must, she felt sure, be an unconscious imitation of the haze of grief hanging over the Professor's verse. Even if there were no actual desire to imitate, it still seemed to her that anything in the way of sorrow must spring from the same abundant source.

It was at this point that she would start to wonder. After living under the same roof for a full ten years, and however the Professor might seek to avoid her in everyday life, she had inevitably developed her own way of viewing things, and come to feel that she knew him better than anyone else. Thus she had personal knowledge of the fact that almost nothing had disturbed the even tenor of his life during those ten years. To some people, a life of such placid monotony—a life, too, free of any particular economic stringency and with a generous supply of adulation—would be a source of envy.

It hardly seemed possible that the grief he distilled from this peaceful life was due solely to a lack of confidence in his own appearance—to his walleye. The world contained any number of men who were uglier than he, with neither ability nor learning, who nevertheless enjoyed perfectly ordinary domestic lives. Why had he, unlike everyone else, clung so obstinately to solitude—deliberately encouraged sorrow—rejected life with such daunting oversensitivity?

At this point in her speculations, she had a strong feeling that if only she could grasp the secret whereby he spun such sophisticated sadness from such a prosaic life, she herself would be able to write poetry worthy of comparison with his. What could the secret be? Suspicion suddenly reared its head, and with a quickening pulse she found her mind straying involuntarily to the most forbidden thoughts. . . .

2

The circumstances described above will doubtless suggest the degree of Tsuneko's surprise when commanded to accompany the Professor on his pilgrimage to the Kumano shrines.

Though the Professor was himself a native of the Kumano district, he had never been back to the village where he was born. There were doubtless reasons to account for this but Tsuneko had never probed into them, and remained none the wiser. On the one occasion when someone claiming to be a relative had visited Tokyo and come calling, the Professor, with almost frightening indifference, had sent the man packing without even showing his face.

Nevertheless, though he always obstinately avoided visiting his birthplace, he had in fact made several trips to Kumano. And now, once more, he had expressed a desire to go: to take advantage of the summer vacation to make a long-deferred pilgrimage to the Three Shrines of Kumano. Moreover this time, it seemed, it was to be a purely private trip, with no lectures or meetings whatever to tie him down.

One advantage of being a scholar was that there was no shortage of young associates willing to look after the house in his absence. So arrangements were made for three of them to stay there, and Tsuneko asked a local caterer to send in meals for them.

The first question that bothered her was what to wear on the journey and what clothes to take with her. The Professor told her, rather irritably, to please herself. So, with no one else to consult, she racked her brains and finally decided to take out some of her savings and have just one new summer kimono made.

Concerning the books she was to bring, however, the Professor was quite specific.

"You'll never be any good at lyric poetry," he said, "so why not use this opportunity to try your hand at descriptive verse? And don't go trying to imitate the modern realistic school. I suggest you study the collected poems of Eifuku Mon'in."

Eifuku Mon'in, of course, was the celebrated poet of the Kamakura period, consort of Fushimi, the ninety-second emperor. A member of the Kyogoku school of verse and as such well represented in the imperial anthology known as the *Gyokuyoshu*, she is noted for descriptive works that display her skill at what Kyogoku Tamekane called "imparting a special fragrance to words." The poem that reads:

> The sun declines
> Behind the eaves,
> The shadows shift
> And fade, linger a while
> On flowers below

was one of which Tsuneko was particularly fond. She hadn't been interested much in the poet to begin with, but under the Professor's influence had come to appreciate the subtle emotion, subtler than that of the average lyric poem, that often lurked in the latter half of what was, in theory, a purely descriptive piece like this.

A volume of Eifuku Mon'in's verse, then. . . . As for clothes, she decided in the end to take her whole store of summer kimonos, since she was likely to sweat. She even took two of her own light cotton kimonos for use inside the hotel, as the Professor was bound to disapprove if she wore the vulgar kind supplied by the management. With one thing or another, her bag swelled steadily.

The Professor, on the other hand, being used to travel, was taking the same battered suitcase as usual, his only extra provisions consisting of an adequate stock of absorbent cotton and a pocket warmer in case he suffered one of his occasional bouts of stomach pain. Ashamed of the size of her own bag, Tsuneko did her best to reduce its contents, but without success.

The three aides who were to look after the house came to stay the night before they left. Saké was served at dinner on the Professor's orders, and the conversation, so far as she could tell, roved in animated fashion over academic topics, travel, and the theater. If only their mentor had been rather more lively, the young men might well have indulged in mild banter on the subject of "second honeymoons." But this, of course, was impossible in the Fujimiya residence; though when even the send-off at Tokyo Station the following morning failed to produce any such jokes, Tsuneko almost began to find it rather unnatural.

The heat that summer was particularly fierce, and by the time the train pulled out at 7:45 the platform was already sweltering.

The send-off party consisted of two of the people who were to look after the house and four students who had got wind of the Professor's departure. Tsuneko, who hitherto had always said goodbye to her master at his front door, shrank from the unaccustomed spotlight of the occasion. In theory, she should have been overwhelmed with joy and a sense of honor, but in fact she felt a twinge of uneasiness: a hint, even, of irrational fear that this journey might be a final gesture preceding her own dismissal.

When a student offered to take her bag, she stubbornly refused, fearing a reprimand, until a "Why not? The young have got energy to spare" from the Professor finally encouraged her to part with it and have it lifted onto the luggage rack for her. In the harsh sunlight that reached to the middle of the platform, the people who'd come to see them off mopped at the dripping sweat. As Assistant Professor Nozoe—who was over thirty and the most senior of the Professor's entourage—said goodbye to Tsuneko, he took it upon himself to add in an aside: "I hope you'll look after him. He gets particularly difficult when he's traveling."

At first, Tsuneko was struck by his thoughtfulness, but on reflection decided that he'd got things the wrong way around. Such parting advice wouldn't have been out of place coming from a wife, but there was no reason why she, who had been attending to the Professor's personal needs for a full ten years, should take it from *him*.

They were all, she suspected, secretly uneasy at the idea of leaving their mentor entirely in her charge, if only for a matter of two or three days. Far from complimenting her on her good fortune, they gave the impression of silently reproaching the Professor for this sudden vagary. It was, after all, a sensational event. . . .

She wished the train would hurry up and leave.

Looking at them out there on the platform, she felt that all of them, personal protégés and ordinary students alike, had something vaguely anachronistic in their manner and appearance that made them conspicuous. Soberly dressed in white short-sleeved shirts and black trousers, they all, down to the youngest student, carried fans in imitation of their patron. The very air with which they swung the fans from cords on their wrists was, precisely, the Professor's. Even Tsuneko, who didn't get out much, knew that today's youngsters didn't carry fans.

At last the train started moving. Although the car they were in had air conditioning, the Professor didn't remove his jacket: he never did so, even in summer.

For a minute or two he sat with his eyes closed, then suddenly opened them as though startled and took the silver container out of his pocket.

The Professor had beautiful hands, as dry and chaste as handmade paper, but the number of dark spots had become increasingly noticeable recently, and constant wiping with alcohol had macerated the fingertips so that they suggested a drowned corpse. It was with such hands that he now took a piece of cotton soaked in alcohol and used it to wipe religiously the armrests, the window ledge, and everywhere else that he might come in contact with. As soon as one piece began to turn black he discarded it, so the container was soon empty.

"I'll make some more," said Tsuneko, intending to replenish it. But the hand she stretched out to get a new supply from the Professor's suitcase on the luggage rack was, quite suddenly, brushed aside in one of the stern, apparently pointless gestures of rejection that she'd observed in him from time to time. She had the impression that, through the relentlessly pervasive aura of alcohol, he had darted a particularly unkind glance at her. The look in his eyes went well with the smell.

The Professor's bad eye was on the left; the eyeball moved even though it couldn't see, so that strangers had the illusion of being looked at with that eye. After ten years in attendance, however, Tsuneko could tell immediately, through the violet spectacles, which way the healthy eye on the right was moving.

To be looked at so coldly after a decade of such personal service was disconcerting: it suggested, somehow, that he regretted bringing her with him almost as soon as they had set out. But Tsuneko was past being shocked. If anything, she was gratified by the suggestion of a spoiled child behaving in the way most natural to it.

She was so busy making swabs with the cotton and alcohol her companion had himself extracted from his bag that they were out of Tokyo before she could pay any attention to the morning scenery she had been looking forward to viewing from the train window. Her task finally finished, she held out the silver container, and waited for him to say something.

"Did you bring the Eifuku Mon'in collection?" he asked eventually, in his high soprano.

"Yes, I did," she replied, taking it from a carrier bag and showing it to him.

"I suggest you pay careful attention to the scenery. I have a feeling this trip will show you what it is you lack. It's partly my own fault, I'm sure, for keeping you shut up in the house all the time, but your recent poems have made me feel that it's time I tried to expand your vision. And you, on your side, must open up your mind, without resistance, to landscapes and nature in general, and remodel your verse without bothering too much about what you've done so far. I don't mean, of course, that you should write a lot of poetry while we're away. You don't need to write. The important thing is to fertilize your poetic sensibility."

"I see. . . . That's very kind of you."

Even as he delivered this homily in his high-pitched voice, the Professor's eyes were surveying Tsuneko restlessly, as though warning her that if he found the slightest trace of grubbiness on the neck of her kimono she would pay for it. Tsuneko, however, was deeply moved by this, the first kindly personal advice she'd had from him as a teacher. Overcome by the idea of his taking so much trouble, she barely managed to get out a "So kind, to bother with someone so hopeless," then was obliged to produce a handkerchief in a hurry and clap it to the brimming tears.

She knew that crying would annoy him, but the tears refused to stop. Yet even as she cried, she was privately reaffirming her determination, before the journey was over, to get at the secret behind his poetic gifts. If only she could put her finger on it, she might actually do something (though the Professor himself might not be too pleased about it) to return the kindness he had shown her.

The Professor took out a book, and from that point until somewhere around Atami devoted himself to reading as though he'd forgotten her very existence.

Kumano could have been reached easily enough by night train, but the Professor, who disliked overnight travel, had chosen to go by day, thanks to which the journey threatened to prove quite a strain. Beyond Nagoya, there wasn't even any air conditioning.

Arriving in Nagoya at noon, they ate lunch in a hotel opposite the station, then after a short rest boarded a diesel-engined semi-express on the Nishi-Kansai line. Even after they were on the train, the memory of the strained atmosphere over lunch lingered, making Tsuneko view with misgiving the prospect of other similar lunches during their trip.

The dining room on the top floor of the hotel, its windows filled entirely by a view of cloudy sky, had been all but deserted. The white tablecloths, even the white napkins, had taken on the gray tinge of the clouds beyond the great glass panes, and Tsuneko felt awkward, not because of any ignorance of Western table manners, but because it didn't feel right to be sitting down opposite the Professor in a formal way like this.

The meal also brought sharply home to her a mistake in her calculations: the more soberly she dressed and the older she tried to appear, the greater in fact was the danger of being mistaken for his wife. As it was, she would have done better to get herself up in a flashier style less appropriate to the circumstances. If only she'd been the type that could wear Western clothes, she could have put on a two-piece suit or something, thus increasing the chances of being taken as his secretary.

The miscalculation, however, was strictly on Tsuneko's side; there was nothing to suggest any such error on the part of the Professor, who had not criticized her appearance when they set out and was still behaving quite agreeably even now. Trying to fathom the workings of his mind, she felt lost again in a fog of incomprehension. Could he perhaps—though it was scarcely imaginable—be deliberately hoping that they would be mistaken for man and wife?

For lunch, the Professor had had cold meat, while Tsuneko had had white fish cooked *à la meunière*. When the coffee came, she held out the silver sugar bowl for him to help himself from first, and as he took it their fingertips came into brief contact. She apologized immediately, but a suspicion plagued her that he had seen the contact as premeditated on her part. It continued to plague her in the maddening heat on the train, so that every time the steady waving of the Professor's fan suddenly stopped her heart seemed to stop with it. She had never reacted in this way before. Perhaps the sense of responsibility she'd felt ever since the train had left Tokyo Station had made her oversensitive? The incident, for which there was no way of apologizing naturally, continued to weigh on her till, combining with the heat, it made it impossible for her to enjoy the scenery outside.

She recalled the sensation as the Professor's fingers had momentarily touched her own. There was nothing really unusual about what had happened; much the same thing must have occurred often enough back at home, at breakfast, on ordinary days. The incident in the hotel, however, had taken place in a large, deserted dining room, before the eyes of several loitering waiters, and the sensation had impressed itself on her with corresponding keenness. It had been—it occurred to her now—like touching the damp petals of a large white magnolia flower, with the cloying scent of a bloom just past its prime.

3

On the first night of the trip, Tsuneko had all kinds of shocking dreams; it must have been tiredness from the long train journey, for she normally prided herself on her ability to sleep soundly. In one particular vision, Professor Fujimiya appeared and chased her in such disgusting form that slumber fled and continued to elude her for some time.

She was in her room in a hot-spring inn in Kii Katsuura, a small room (separate, of course, from the Professor's) built out over the sea so that one could hear the sound of the water furtively lapping the shore below. Listening to it in the darkness, she had a feeling that small animals, smacking their chops and jostling each other, were crawling up the wooden supports beneath the building. But, frightened and trembling though she was, she must have gone off to sleep again, for she was still in bed long after her usual hour on the following morning.

She was woken by the ringing of the telephone. It was the Professor, to say that he was already up. Her clock said half past six, and the room was full of morning sunlight. Leaping hastily out of bed, she washed, rapidly dressed herself, and went to the Professor in his room.

"Good morning to you." The greeting was casual; but just at that moment she caught sight of what seemed to be the edge of something in a purple crepe wrapping cloth, clumsily concealed beneath the table. She must have been too quick getting ready, and have unintentionally surprised him in the act of looking over some private documents. If so, it was hardly her own fault, but she disliked the suggestion of snooping; she considered withdrawing again, but felt it would look too self-conscious, and gave up the idea.

"It seems you slept well," said the Professor—who had already dyed his hair and shaved—in a benign soprano. His voice in the early morning had a special flutelike clarity, almost like the warbling of a bird.

"Yes, thank you. I'm very sorry. I overslept."

"Never mind. It's a good thing to lie in occasionally. But you ought to be a little more considerate. It doesn't do to get flurried and rush to my room in a panic. It's hardly as though I'd had a stroke and needed you to hurry as much as that. In a case like this, you should say you're sorry quietly, over the telephone, tell me in a normal fashion how many minutes you'll take, then get ready in a leisurely way and come along at the time you said. That's the proper way for a woman to behave."

"Yes, of course. I'm really very sorry."

"There's no need to apologize. Just be more careful in future. There's a passage in *Advice for Actors* that says, 'to seek to take everything upon oneself, ignoring the others concerned, is referred to disparagingly as "going it alone." ' It's a useful warning for anyone, not just the actor. After all, service to others must always be calculated to fit the particular situation."

"Yes, of course. I'll try to be more careful. It was stupid of me."

To be grumbled at in this way did not, oddly enough, annoy Tsuneko. On the contrary, it gave her the illusion of being somehow small and cute, as though she'd turned into a meek little girl again. And the suggestion that their situation was special, unlike the way things were done in ordinary society, heightened the sense of satisfaction still further. For example, it was often said that young girls working in department stores nowadays would quit if they were told off, however mildly. For her, though, provided she kept her pride and her confidence in the idea that she was indispensable, to be scolded was if anything a pleasure. . . .

Even as she entertained these thoughts, Tsuneko was not entirely free of a desire to peer into the forbidden depths of the Professor's mind. Was his severity a form of fatherly affection, or was it simply objective criticism? If her behavior really bothered him so much, why didn't he get rid of her, instead of going out of his way to bring her with him on this journey?

"I've asked them to get us a boat," said the Professor after a while.

Tsuneko took the cue to go out on the veranda and gaze at the scenery. The sea was already dazzling in the midsummer light, but this was a landlocked bay, and not a single wave was to be seen in the vicinity. On the near side of Nakanoshima island, which lay directly ahead, rows of pearl cultivation rafts floated on the water, while to the left, at the northern extremity of the bay, lay a harbor from which the constant thud of ships' engines was audible. The hills on the opposite side of the bay were wrapped in an almost unnaturally dark green; a cable car ran up to their summit, about two hundred and fifty feet above sea level, and she could see where the green had been stripped away around the observation platform, revealing the red earth.

The bay opened to the south. On the horizon beyond, clouds in clusters lay emulating islands, and far out toward it the sea, shadowed by the clouds above, was like a pallid face.

Tsuneko had the sense not to gush about lovely scenery and the like, yet she was, after all, a poet in her own small way, and here, faced with this morning seascape, she felt the long years in the dark dwelling in Hongo suddenly dwindling to the merest speck of soot, and took a deep breath as though to draw in for future reference as much as possible of the view before her eyes.

At this point a maid brought in the small tables bearing their breakfasts.

"Oh—I'll see to things for the Professor," said Tsuneko so that the maid, who was supposed to serve them rice and tea toward the end, wouldn't hover over them during the meal.

She'd deliberately emphasized the "Professor" to make their relationship quite clear; she was afraid this would seem officious again, but fortunately the Professor made no comment.

After breakfast and before the boat left, however, they did have a spot of bother. The management sent along someone with several square decorated cards of the kind on which distinguished guests are expected to write something to commemorate their visit. This made the Professor rather cross, and Tsuneko was obliged to go to the manager and explain, apologetically, that he had no time for that sort of thing.

The Professor had hired a small sightseeing boat for their own exclusive use. They left the harbor, crossing waters that were green and soupy in the shadow of the islands, and set off around the coast to the west. The voice of the hotel clerk, who had joined them on board as their guide, reached them only fitfully, bawling above the sound of the engine, so that Tsuneko could hardly tell which was which of the oddly shaped rocks he was identifying.

There was a "Lion Rock," with several pine trees growing on it that were supposed to be represent the mane, and a "Camel Rock," with two humps. Dotted here and there in the open sea where the waves were noticeably higher than in the bay, the rocky islets had a smugness about them that Tsuneko personally found rather tiresome. Uninhabited, they sat there for inspection, though with half their forms hidden underwater, silently content to be given labels that were appropriate or not according to how you looked at them; most so-called beauty spots, she supposed, were the same. They reminded her of her own past: even the term "married couple," it occurred to her now, had been a pretense no more grounded in actuality than the lion and the camel. Compared with such relationships, her life with the Professor was a reality that no name could ever hope to define:

not some half-submerged rock, not something just squatting there to be stared at. . . .

Taking in a view of a cape beyond which, they were told, lay a stretch of deep water where whales were often caught, the vessel turned back to the east and, reaching the entrance to the bay, passed through an awe-inspiring cave that pierced a particularly large and magnificent rock known as "the Crane."

The Professor, who was holding on tightly to the side of the boat, was clearly enjoying his trip, in the way a child would do.

He was fond of danger provided it was on a limited scale, not too serious, and incurred in a spirit of play. To him, she suspected, even the soft slaps that the thrusting waves dealt the underside of the boat as it went through the cave felt like small, personal gestures of revenge for a long and somber life of study. It must have been gratifying to feel these little counter-shocks disturbing—stirring into a flurry—the dark, still waters that had gathered in his mind after endless brooding on the more stable shore.

With these thoughts, Tsuneko kept her eyes resolutely on the seascape, refraining from addressing the Professor until finally an increasing number of fantastically shaped rocks to the east, clustered around a distant promontory and wrapped in the haze hanging over the sea, happened to suggest to her the legendary home of the Taoist Immortals and, breaking her silence at last, she said:

"I wonder where we're going."

It had suddenly seemed to her as if the boat, with the Professor and herself on board, was bearing them toward some utopian land—was approaching, after long adversity and suffering, a world in which ugliness no longer had any part. Where appearances were concerned, she had always been sensitive to the Professor's and her own shortcomings. They would never be taken for a handsome pair: to link them erotically in the mind was to make imagination look the other way. In bringing her along, the Professor had almost certainly been aware of this. And just as certainly he had had it borne home on him again and again, in the course of his sixty years, that in a love affair the plaudits of the onlookers are almost as important as the sincere feelings of the principals. Being twice as sensitive as other men, and a lover of beauty into the bargain, he probably felt that the times he spent alone with Tsuneko, seated at the very stern of life, were the only times when he could relax: relax in the knowledge that, having no part in beauty, he was in no danger of doing it any injury.

It was thus, sitting far astern, that the pair of them were sailing toward the promised land. . . .

Though it was unlikely that he had followed Tsuneko's train of thought quite as far as this, the Professor was not one to let her brief question as to where they were going pass lightly. A more conventional man might have answered with a "Where? I imagine we'll just do the sights, then go back to where we started." Instead, a slight irritation flashed somewhere behind his violet spectacles, as though he feared entanglement in some tiresome vagary of the female psyche. Being quite used to such wariness, and quite prepared to respect it, Tsuneko hastened to explain the reason for her question:

"I mean—it was just that the scenery over there reminded me somehow of the Land of the Immortals, and I had a feeling that the boat was taking us straight in that direction."

"Why, yes, of course. 'Land of the Immortals'—how very apt. The way the mist hangs over everything suggests exactly that. And in fact, of course, Kumano always has been closely associated with the Taoist Immortals. Admittedly, the only home of theirs I know of that's actually in the sea is Horai. . . ."

172

Which wasn't exactly a warm response, but Tsuneko, of course, had only herself to blame.

Just at that moment, the hotel clerk pointed toward the shore and shouted:

"Look, over there! D'you see the vertical white line to the left of Mt. Myoho? That's the Nachi Falls. They say this is the only spot in the whole of Japan where you can view a waterfall from the sea like this. So you'd better take a good look."

Sure enough, on the dark green right-hand slope of Mt. Myoho there was a place where the bare earth of the mountain was visible and, set against it, what looked like a pillar of white, unpainted wood. Tsuneko looked hard, and it almost seemed that the single white line was quivering slightly and climbing jerkily upward, though it might have been that the haze over the sea created a distorted mirage of motion.

A thrill passed through her.

If it was indeed the Nachi Falls, what they were doing was like stealing a forbidden look at some deity from a distant vantage point. By rights, of course, one ought to stand gazing up in awe at the waterfall from the edge of its basin; but the deity of the fall might be so used to stretching up its noble form high above men's heads that for a moment it had grown careless, thus allowing human eyes out at sea this total view of itself, endearingly small in the distance.

This induced in turn the fanciful notion that they had caught a forbidden glimpse of a goddess bathing. Yes—Tsuneko now decided—the deity of the waterfall was, quite definitely, a nymph.

Whether the Professor would go along with such fancies she wasn't sure; feeling it inappropriate to disclose them just now, she decided to make a poem out of them sometime later and submit it for his approval.

"Well, then, shall we get back to the inn?" he said. "We can

173

go out and pay our respects to the waterfall later. I never get tired of seeing the Nachi Falls. A visit there always leaves me feeling spiritually purified."

He was gripping the side of the boat uneasily as he spoke, holding himself slightly clear of the incessantly rocking seat in the stern—though this time, perhaps because he trusted in the disinfecting properties of sea breezes, he had brought none of his cotton swabs on board.

Tsuneko herself felt glad at this evidence that the Professor was enjoying the journey; for it was clear, even to a bystander, what a strain the work of a great scholar was. On the one hand, the ever-present danger that the discovery of a single piece of long-forgotten material might suddenly upset a whole fabric of theory meant that a structure built up boldly on intuition—providing the intuition kept a sharp eye on the future—was, in principle at least, longer lasting. Yet on the other hand this approach was, in itself, in constant danger of lapsing into either poetry or art. The Professor had spent his whole life walking the fine tightrope between poetic intuition and documentary evidence. There had been times, of course, when the former approach had been correct and others, presumably, when it hadn't; yet it seemed safe to say that it had been right more often than the documentary one. The long, solemn struggle he had waged, unseen, in his study was something beyond Tsuneko's powers of apprehension. Nevertheless, however clear the inner vision attained there through the honing and refining of intellect and intuition, she could still guess at a fatigue transcending the human will, a fatigue that had taken its toll both physically and spiritually. It might be that, when a person strove too hard to apprehend something outside himself, some kind of exchange occurred eventually between him and the object of his interest, leaving him subtly altered. Possibly, even, it

174

was an intuitive sense of this state of affairs that had led ignorant students to label the Professor "Dr. Weirdo."

All in all, Tsuneko told herself, it was a very good thing that a man like this should get away from it all; and it was understandable too that he should have chosen—lest fresh and over-stimulating impressions tire him—a place that he had visited before. And she began to feel that rather than drag him back spiritually to the confines of his study by being oversensitive to his moods, it might be better for her to make mindless conversation designed to take the tension out of him.

However well meant, when a woman like Tsuneko conceives a plan of this sort, it is bound to seem artificial and clumsy in the realization. In the car after they left the hotel on the way to Nachi, she rejoiced aloud over the fact that the car was air-conditioned:

"How thoughtful of them," she said. "Why—even in Tokyo you don't get air-conditioned taxis! In the old days, I suppose, people visited the waterfall partly because it was so cool there, but nowadays you can actually get cool on the way. It makes you feel a bit spoiled, doesn't it? And there was I in Tokyo, every time you went on a trip, worrying about how tiring it must be for you, when in fact it seems quite comfortable. . . ."

This, and more of the same, was designed of course to draw the Professor out, to make him take pity on her ignorance and facile conjectures, and talk to her of the hardships of travel undertaken in the cause of scholarship.

But he was not one to react in any such commonplace way just because he happened to be away from home. Gently, he allowed his eyes to close. Tsuneko worried for a moment in case he felt ill, but it seemed this wasn't so.

The eyes, closed behind the pale mauve lenses, were surrounded by a mass of wrinkles, so that it was difficult to make out where the line of the eyelids stopped and the wrinkles started. His ability to shut out the outside world at a moment's notice reminded her of certain kinds of insect. At the same time, it meant that she had a rare opportunity to scrutinize him from close to. In doing so, it occurred to her that she was inspecting his face thoroughly for the first time in ten years; until now, she'd done no more than cast timid glances up at it from lowered eyes.

The sunlight flickering through the car window showed where flecks of undissolved black dye had left dark smudges at the hairline. Seeing them, she felt that it wouldn't have happened if only he had left things to her; it came of his insisting on doing things alone, using his one good eye. Seen close up, his looks weren't really so terrible; the unprepossessing appearance for which he was famous was due mainly to the bad proportions of his body as a whole and the incongruity of his voice. In fact, the small and gently curving mouth had a boyish freshness surprising in a man of sixty. If only he would stop being stubborn and let a woman look after what he wore, there was no telling what a dapper new Professor might be made of him. . . .

At this point in her speculations a sixth sense born of long years' experience made her swiftly avert her gaze and assume an unconcerned expression, so that when the Professor opened his eyes he seemed totally unaware that until a moment before he had been under such intense scrutiny.

The Nachi Falls had been one of the nation's holy sites throughout the two thousand years since the emperor Jimmu had first accorded it divine status and worshiped it as Oana-muchi-no-kami (another name for Okuninushi-no-kami). There had been eighty-three imperial visits, beginning with that of the retired emperor Uda, and the emperor Kazan had done a thousand days' personal penance beneath the fall.

176

The spot, moreover, had been celebrated as a center of ascetic practices ever since En-no-gyoja had first thought to stand beneath its cold waters as a form of spiritual discipline. The waterfall had been dubbed Hiro Gongen—the "Flying Water Bodhisattva"—and the building that stood by it was still known officially as the "Flying Water Shrine."

"One doesn't really need to know anything about it in advance in order to appreciate it," said the Professor without lifting his head from the back of his seat, speaking in the monotonous, lethargic tone he used for his lectures. "But to approach it with the benefit of some knowledge should add to its interest.

"I think you had better know something at least about the origins of popular worship at the Three Shrines of Kumano.

"As one might expect of a site dedicated originally to Okuninushi-no-kami, the Kumano shrines seem to have been closely linked with the Izumo people, and despite the remoteness of their location they were already well known in the time of the *Chronicles of Japan*. The prevalence of densely wooded, gloomy mountains inspired the idea that the spot gave access to the land of the dead. In later ages, these ancient associations with the nether world came to overlap with a belief in the Pure Land of Kannon, thus giving rise to the peculiar form of faith associated with Kumano.

"The three shrines were originally independent of each other, but over the years all kinds of beliefs became amalgamated into one, and their histories and the gods they enshrined were unified, leading eventually to their being venerated as a trinity.

"Rites of national significance were performed here as early as the Nara period, and Buddhist ceremonies were often held in front of the Shinto gods. A reference in the *Kegon Sutra* to Fudaraku, the Pure Land of Kannon, as being 'on a mountain ly-

177

ing to the south' led people to suppose that it was somewhere on a southern coast. Thus it came to be identified with the coastal region that included the Nachi Falls, and people began to worship there in the hope of attaining prosperity and happiness."

So the coast as they had seen it earlier from the boat, with the Nachi Falls behind it, had been a prospect of the Pure Land itself! What strange chance of fate was it—wondered Tsuneko—that she should have seen the paradise of Kannon on the very first morning of this curious journey?

"The identification of native Shinto gods with the divinities of Buddhism thus gave rise to the idea that the waterfall was a manifestation of the Bodhisattva Kannon. Subsequently, however, in the late Heian period, the popular belief that the deity represented in the main shrine's Shojoden was in fact the Buddha Amida got the better of the view of Nachi as the Pure Land of Kannon; and the contemporary preoccupation with rebirth in the Pure Land of Amida, fostered by a growing belief that the age of the Buddhist Law was in decline, created a fashion at the shrines for the rigorous ascetic practices of which the three years' penance done by the cloistered emperor Kazan was just one example.

"In time, administration of the three shrines passed into the hands of the Buddhist priesthood; a type of itinerant ascetic called *yamabushi* appeared, and there emerged the cult known as Shugendo, which combined service to the Shinto gods with ascetic Buddhist observances in remote mountain settings. . . ."

The Professor's lecture seemed likely to go on for some time, but she was retaining, as she listened, only those parts that promised to be useful in her verse.

It was puzzling that, though undoubtedly brought up here in Kumano, he was just as undoubtedly determined to avoid his birthplace. Perhaps the reason lay in what she had just heard—

in the region's associations with eternal night, in its suggestions of a land of the dead, a gloomy nether world of dark green shadow, which had made him long for yet fear it at the same time and had brought him here again on this journey. His own personal qualities, certainly, were quite appropriate to someone born in such a haunted region. But wasn't it possible too that, for all his resistance to the living world, he had left behind in the deep green Pure Land of this district something of beauty, something that, albeit anxiously, he was hoping to make his own again?...

Tsuneko was still toying with these thoughts when the car drew up in front of the gateway of the Nachi sanctuary. They got out of the air-conditioned vehicle, shrinking from the blast of heat that struck their faces, and set off down the stone steps leading to the adjacent sub-shrine, where the sunlight pouring through the trees lay copiously like hot snow.

By now the Nachi Falls was directly before them. The single sacred staff of gold erected on a rock shone brilliantly as it caught the distant spray; its gilded form, set bravely in opposition to the waterfall, appeared and disappeared in the smoke from a mass of burning incense sticks.

Catching sight of the Professor, the shrine's chief priest came up and greeted him with obvious respect, then showed them to a spot close to the pool formed at its base, where ordinary visitors were not allowed because of the danger of falling rocks. The great black lock on the red-lacquered gate was rusty and refused to open at first; once they were inside, the path led perilously over rocks till it came to the pool's edge.

Settling herself with difficulty on a flattish stone, where the fine spray fell pleasantly on her face, Tsuneko raised her eyes to the waterfall, so close now that it seemed to pour onto her breast.

It was no longer a nymph; it was a huge, fierce-looking male god.

Ceaselessly, the torrent slid its white foam over a rockface that was like a polished metal mirror. High above its crest a summer cloud showed its dazzling brow, and a single, withered cryptomeria thrust its sharp needle into the blue sky's eye. Halfway down, the foam, striking the rock, shattered in all directions, so that as she gazed she felt that the wall of rock itself was crumbling, bulging forward, and coming down on top of her; if she bent her head and looked sideways, she could almost fancy that the places where water and rock collided were spurting countless springs in unison. The lower halves of rockface and water stood almost completely apart, so that one could clearly see the shadow of the fall rushing down the mirror-surface of the stone.

The torrent gathered breezes about it. On the nearby hillside, trees, grass, and bamboo thicket waved in the constant wind, shining with a dangerous-looking sharpness where they had caught the spray. With a rim of sunlight around their foliage, the restless trees had a wild and desperate air that was uniquely beautiful. "Like madwomen in the Noh," thought Tsuneko.

Before she realized it her ears had got so used to the roaring all around her that she was quite oblivious to it. Only when she stared, absorbed, into the still, deep green waters of the basin did the sound, perversely, revive in her ears. The profound sluggishness of the pool's surface was broken only by sharp-edged ripples like a pond in heavy rain.

"This is the first time I've seen such a splendid waterfall," she said, and bowed her head slightly in gratitude for having been brought to see it.

"For you, everything is the first time," the Professor answered in a tinkling voice, without turning from his position standing directly facing the cascade.

The voice had never sounded to her so mysterious, or so spitefully disparaging.

Could he be taunting her as being, spiritually at least, a total innocent, even though he knew that she'd been married? Surely it was excessively unkind to imply that someone was an innocent at forty-five? She might be an attendant at the Fujimiya shrine, but why should he mock the very purity that he himself insisted on?

"Shall we go?" she found herself saying, getting up to match the suggestion. As she did so, her foot slipped on the mossy rock; she started to fall, and at that instant, with the unexpected swiftness of a young man, the Professor thrust out a hand to help her. For less than a moment Tsuneko hesitated, uncertain whether to take the pale, antiseptic hand held out to her.

The hand floated in the roar of the waterfall, a divine apparition threatening abduction to lands unknown. A large magnolia flower loomed before her eyes, its petals elegantly freckled and sweet-smelling.... But her body was in danger of losing its balance and falling on the slippery rock. Finally she submitted, yielding to the enticement, aware that it was illusion even to consider it as such, yet in a state of pleasant giddiness that bordered on a swoon.

Unfortunately, the Professor's strength was not up to the burden. When she took hold of him, he started to fall in turn. If they had both staggered and collapsed onto the rocks, they might have been seriously injured. But an instant sense of the Professor's importance made Tsuneko brace her legs, and with great difficulty she just managed to keep him up.

As they straightened up, they were both panting and flushed

in the face. The Professor's spectacles were in danger of slipping off, and she hastily set them to rights for him; it was a gesture that at ordinary times he would surely have repulsed, but now he merely said "Thank you" in a voice suffused with embarrassment. He couldn't have made Tsuneko happier.

4

It was an odd summer morning: one on which, without conscious design, all kinds of bonds were loosened and many taboos lifted. Probably the Professor himself was not particularly aware of having lifted them, but had simply felt like letting things take their own course for once.

To pay one's respects at the Nachi Grand Shrine, repository of the divine spirit of the Nachi Falls, it was necessary to climb, in the full heat of the summer sun, a flight of more than four hundred stone steps. Since the climb was grueling enough to make one sweat profusely even in spring and autumn, only a handful of people ever thought of taking it on at the height of summer and at this time of day. Young people nowadays must have weak legs, Tsuneko reflected, for she noticed boys and girls who were ready to give up after the first few dozen steps; she looked at them quizzically, only to find herself in trouble once they were past the first resting place on the way.

The Professor climbed in silence, ignoring the resting places with their promise of refreshments, rejecting Tsuneko's helping hand. It was a mystery where such stamina had been lurking in him. He let Tsuneko carry the jacket of his suit, but refused to buy a walking stick, pressing on through the reflected heat with not enough breeze even to belly out his unfashionably wide-cut trousers, lifting himself doggedly from one step to the next, his steeply sloping shoulders bent forward, his gait swaying as ever. The back of his shirt was already soaked with sweat, but he wouldn't allow himself to use his fan or do anything more than mop the sweat dripping from his forehead with the hand-kerchief clasped in his hand. His profile as he flogged himself on, head bent, eyes fixed on the bleached surface of the steps, bore noble suggestions of a life spent in the solitary pursuit of knowledge and at the same time, typically, suggested a desire to let people see the suffering inherent in his solitude. It was a pain-ful sight that left, like the salt left after seawater has evaporated, a trace of the sublime.

Watching him, Tsuneko could not bring herself to complain on her own behalf. Her heart felt as though it was thrusting up into her throat, her knees hurt with the unaccustomed exercise, her calves were painful, and her legs grew more and more unsteady, as though she were walking on clouds. Worst of all was the infernal heat. Her head swam, she seemed likely to faint from fatigue—and yet, as time went by, something pure seemed to well up out of the depths of the fatigue, like fresh water springing from sandy soil. Perhaps, it occurred to her, it was only at moments like this—only after this kind of hardship—that one achieved with any real sense of conviction a vision of the Pure Land of Kumano of which the Professor had spoken in the car. It was a land of mysterious shadow, sheltered by the cool green cover of trees, a land where there was no sweat, where one's chest never hurt. . . .

And there, perhaps—the idea came into her mind, and promptly became a stick for her to cling to, giving her the cour-age to go on climbing—there, perhaps, it was fated that the Pro-fessor and she should cast off restraint and come together in all their purity. For ten years, although the hope had never once been consciously acknowledged, she had dreamed of mutual respect exalted into no ordinary love, but a sublime love that dwelt in the shade of old cedars deep in the mountains. It would not be the commonplace love of ordinary men and women; nor would it be the mutual vaunting of good looks that sometimes passed for love. The Professor and she would come to each other as two transparent pillars of light, in some spot where they could look down with scorn on the people on earth below. And perhaps that spot lay at the top of these very steps up which she was now toiling.

Deaf to the singing of the cicadas all about, blind to the green of the cedars crowding both sides of the steps, she went on, aware of nothing but the sunlight, a kind of dizziness in itself, beating down directly on the nape of her neck, till she reached a stage where she seemed to be tottering along in a billowing, luminous haze.

But when they reached the precincts of the Nachi Grand Shrine and she had splashed cold water from the font on her hair, moistened her throat, and finally relaxed enough to look around her at the scene, it was no Pure Land she saw but brightly lit reality.

The broad view was bounded by mountains, Eboshi-ga-take and Hikari-ga-mine to the north and the summits of Mt. Myoho to the south; skirting the coniferous woods below, they could see the bus road to Myoho, where there was a temple enshrining the hair of the dead. A single break in the hills to the east gave a glimpse of the sea: present reminder of the sense of awe that the sun, rising in the gap and wondrously transforming the dark mountains, must have inspired in men of old. Like an arrow of rose-colored, life-giving light released with a sudden twang into the land of the dead, its rays would effortlessly have pierced the solemn banks of mist that were always said to lie about the mountains of Kumano, the haze described in the tenth book of the *Tales of the Heike* as "the compassionate mists of grace". . . .

Here again Professor Fujimiya was on friendly terms with the chief priest, and they were shown through a red-lacquered lattice gateway into the inner garden.

The main deity of this shrine was Fusumi-no-okami (another name for Izanami-no-omikami) but, as was the peculiarity of all three Kumano shrines, the most important deities of the other two sites were venerated here as well. Thus when they entered the courtyard they could see six buildings—Takimiya, Shojo-den, Naka-no-gozen, Nishi-no-gozen (the main sanctuary), Waka-miya, and Hasshinden—standing in a row, the shape of each structure, the very tiles of its roof, giving expression to the masculine power or feminine grace of the god or goddess enshrined within. The old saying was right when it claimed that "the very mountains defend the faith": Kumano was a special religious realm where gods and Buddhas jostled each other for space.

Beneath the summer sun, the shrine buildings and the rich verdure of cedar-covered hills behind created a brilliant contrast of vermilion and green.

With an amiable "Take your time, won't you," the chief priest went off, leaving them in sole possession of the inner garden with its celebrated old weeping cherry tree and its rock shaped like a raven. In the heat, even the moss had a whitish, fuzzy look. The garden lay hushed: one could almost hear the gods breathing softly as they took their noontide nap.

"Look—," said the Professor, pointing to the six shrine roofs visible beyond a tall wooden fence, "the 'frog's-leg' brackets in the eaves are all different."

But Tsuneko was too struck by something uneasy in the Professor's own manner to look in the direction he indicated. Although he'd wiped off the sweat and neatly donned his jacket so that he looked positively cool, with no sign of the hardships of a while ago, he had somehow acquired a vaguely harassed expression. His gaze, too, roved restlessly around the roots of the trees nearby. About to ask him whether he had dropped something, Tsuneko checked herself abruptly.

For just at this point, he set her heart beating fast by carefully drawing from his pocket the object in a purple wrapping cloth that she had glimpsed that morning. Apparently unconcerned that she was watching, he proceeded to untie the cloth, revealing a lining of dazzling white silk on which lay three decorative combs made of boxwood, every detail down to the delicate carving of Chinese bellflowers plainly visible in the fierce sunlight.

The sheer elegance of these objects produced a strong reaction in Tsuneko, who simultaneously had caught sight of three Chinese characters inscribed in red with a writing brush, one on each of the combs.

One was a character that could be read *ko* or *ka*.

One, though she wasn't certain, looked like *yo*.

One was probably *ko*.

A single glance was not enough to be quite sure, but it was a safe guess that, taken together, they made up a woman's name: Kayoko. Moreover, the three vermilion characters, written in what looked suspiciously like the Professor's hand, had such an extreme feminine grace that they imprinted themselves as unmistakably on her mind as if she had caught a brief glimpse of some dignified lady in the nude. Though they were done in the square, formal style, each stroke was executed with a delicacy and loving care that told of the intense feeling with which the Professor had wielded the brush. Almost certainly the woman of the mysterious red characters had been lurking in her soft bed of white-lined cloth ever since the start of their trip. Tsuneko couldn't help resenting the fact that all through the journey so far the Professor had been concealing from her this, the only woman's name with which he'd been personally associated during the past ten years. Quite suddenly, the Pure Land she had been busily picturing to herself throughout that long, sweat-drenched climb vanished, leaving her—not in heaven—but in hell; for the first time in her life, Tsuneko was jealous.

Although the episode might seem to have lasted quite a while, in fact the Professor exposed the set of three combs to Tsuneko's eyes for only the briefest of moments before taking out the one inscribed with *ka*, wrapping the others up carefully in the cloth again, and putting them away in his pocket.

"I have to get this buried somewhere, quickly. Find me a good place near the roots of a tree. Somewhere where it'll be easy to dig a hole."

"Yes, of course." Even as she spoke, Tsuneko pitied herself for the way sheer habit made her, despite her own distress, comply instantly with his command. Though her mind resisted, her eyes were already searching the garden.

"I wonder if the foot of that weeping cherry wouldn't be best."

"Yes. A good idea. Particularly in the spring, under the blossom . . ."

And with almost indecent haste he went up to the tree, knelt at its roots, gently removed the fuzz of moss, then began vigorously scraping out the soil underneath with his nails. This was unlike his usual antiseptic self, but perhaps he considered that sacred soil was free of germs.

In an instant, the comb had vanished into the earth, and the graceful red inscription with it. With Tsuneko's help, he neatly replaced the moss to hide any sign of the ground having been disturbed. Then, still on his knees, he joined his hands briefly in prayer—and immediately looked about him to check that no one was coming, an action that somehow suggested less the Professor she was used to than someone guilty of a crime.

Eventually, trying to look casual, he got to his feet and, taking a cleaning pad from another pocket, proceeded to wipe his fingers assiduously, giving another piece to Tsuneko for the same purpose. It was the first time he'd ever shared his pads with her. And as she carefully cleaned the dirt from her nails, with the cool, businesslike smell of the alcohol in her nostrils, she had the feeling that all unwittingly she'd been made an accomplice in this little crime.

5

They spent that night at Shingu. The following day they were to visit the Hayatama Shrine in the morning, then take a car to the Nimasu Shrine, in Motomiya-machi, in the afternoon. With that, their triple pilgrimage to the shrines of Kumano would be accomplished.

But ever since the affair of the combs Tsuneko had taken to dwelling on her own thoughts. She continued to do as the Professor said but, even though they were still on their journey, the new, cheerful self had disappeared, replaced by a Tsuneko in no way different from the one who inhabited the gloomy interior of the residence in Hongo.

Since the shrine visits were scheduled for the morrow, they returned to the inn once they had done the sights of Shingu. There was nothing more to do that day, so Tsuneko took out the collection of Eifuku Mon'in's verse that she had brought with her, with the aim of spending the time till dinner reading. Officially, the Professor too was reading in his own room, though she suspected he was taking a nap.

In her heart, she felt bitter toward him—a feeling sustained by the fact that, despite her obvious depression, he had still made no reference to the combs. It wasn't, of course, the kind of subject she could bring up herself, so, until the Professor broached it from his side, she was left to brood on the riddle alone.

Tsuneko had rarely looked into the mirror even when completely alone in the house in Hongo, but now she did so whenever she had an idle moment by herself. The mirror here, on a cheap red-lacquered stand of the kind often found in such rooms, was quite adequate for inspecting a face with so few pretensions.

Not surprisingly, the book had no portrait of Eifuku Mon'in in it, and there was no way of guessing what she had looked like, but it was doubtful that her face had been anything like her own, with its small eyes, its scraggy cheeks and fleshless earlobes and, worse still, its slightly protruding teeth. No, in every respect—material circumstances, social status, physical appearance—the woman had been utterly different from herself. Why then had the Professor told her to read the poems?

Born the eldest daughter of Saionji Sanekane, the Chief Minister of the day, the poet had gone into service at court at the age of eighteen. She had been appointed a lady-in-waiting, then had gone on to become second consort to the emperor Fushimi. When the emperor abdicated to become a Buddhist monk, she had been given a new name, Eifuku Mon'in. On the death of the retired emperor, she took holy orders, at the age of forty-six, with the Buddhist name of Shinnyogen. Thereafter, while devoting herself to the study of Buddhism, she became the leading female poet of the Kyogoku school of *tanka*, under the patronage of the next emperor, Hanazono. The turbulence of the Kemmu Restoration left her declining years undisturbed, and she finally died at the age of seventy-two.

Hers was a politically difficult period, with the imperial house split into two opposing lines. Her last years in particular saw the rebellion of Ashikaga Takauji, followed by the Kemmu Restoration and the age of the Northern and Southern Courts. Yet her poetry remained unaffected by political and social developments, diligently pursuing its task of framing a delicate observation of nature in a language of great grace and subtle nuance. She never once forgot the injunction, traditionally ascribed to Teika, to compose verse "with compassion and a sense of the sorrow of existence."

One thing that troubled Tsuneko was the fact that Eifuku Mon'in had taken the tonsure when she was only one year older than she herself was at present: could the Professor be hinting that she, too, ought to become a nun a year from now?

Nor was that all. The period when the poet's work was at its most exquisitely beautiful, the very epitome of the style of the *Gyokuyoshu* anthology to which she was such an important contributor, corresponded precisely with her forties. In 1313, when the anthology was completed and presented to the emperor for inspection, she would have been forty-three. This meant that such highly effective specimens of the *Gyokuyoshu* style of natural description as:

> Chillier still
> The wind, blowing,
> Brings mingled snow
> In this cold twilit sky
> Of spring rain

and:

> Where the hills begin
> The song of birds
> Heralds the dawn;

First here, then there,
The blossom takes on color

were composed when she was around the age that Tsuneko was now.

It seemed unlikely even so that, until the death in later years of the emperor Fushimi, Eifuku Mon'in ever experienced any real emotional pain. Perhaps the idea that art was born only of suffering was an erroneous modern assumption? If so, then the Professor might only be trying to tell her, encouragingly, that first-rate poetry could be produced even out of her own emotional doldrums—which would mean, too, that she was badly off the mark in trying to ferret out the secret of his own sadness, stirring up feelings where there was no need for them.

Under any government and in any society, for beautiful scenery to produce beautiful verse surely required that the poet, if a woman, should have beauty and position in the manner of Eifuku Mon'in, or, if a man, some strong, unshakable ideas of his own. And every time the elegance of a particular poem by Eifuku Mon'in impressed her strongly, she would feel her own hopeless lack of qualifications to write such verse, making her want to throw the book, which the Professor had been good enough to lend her, down on the floor. Then, having indeed thrown it down, she would feel she had been horribly disloyal to him—and pick it up again, only to find that just holding it was almost more than she could bear.

All she could see in it was a book crammed with the surface brilliance of a superficial woman—unfeeling, unnecessarily decorative lines devoid of both joy and sadness. What, she wondered, would one of the Professor's male associates do if he felt the same way as she did now? Probably, she decided, he would dash himself against his mentor like an angry wave (though one, of course, that observed the proprieties), and the latter would meet this spiritual upheaval with mildness and tolerance.

Abruptly, she left the room with the book clasped to her breast. Trotting along the corridor, she knelt in the approved fashion before the sliding doors of the Professor's room and called:

"May I come in?"

"Do," came the mild, high-pitched voice from the other side of the doors, a voice that might have been either a man's or a woman's. She went in.

As she'd feared, the Professor was seated at a low table in front of an electric fan, reading a thick volume whose fluttering pages he held down with one finger.

"I've come to return the book you kindly lent me."

"Have you finished it, then?"

"Yes, well . . . no."

"You don't have to give it back till you've finished it. Why don't you keep it till the end of the trip?"

"I see."

She could tell that her equivocal answers were irritating him. Afraid of a scolding, she suddenly bowed low on the tatami:

"Professor—I can't write poetry any more."

"Why?" he asked, with the calm of extreme surprise.

"It's no use. However hard I work at it, I . . . Someone like me . . ."

Before she could finish, the first real tears she had ever shed in the Professor's presence came welling up.

One might almost have thought he had been looking forward to precisely this kind of eventuality, which he could never have borne at normal times, as one of the pleasures of the journey. For an unexpectedly childlike, almost roguish twinkle appeared in the depths of the mauve spectacles, even though his tone was

192

solemn and his face reproving as he said:

"Now listen to me. You mustn't give up halfway. I thought you were the sort of person who almost never got emotional, but the lesson to be learned from Eifuku Mon'in is the importance in art of concealing one's emotions. Even the kind of poetry that is usually considered 'subjective art' is in no way an exception. Modern verse has lost sight of this basic principle. I myself have been corrupted by modern poetry into writing the kind of verse I do, which is why I recommended that collection to you—to keep you from repeating my own mistake. So you mustn't let it have the opposite effect like this.

"Eifuku Mon'in reveals nothing directly in her work, but—" He turned the pages of the book that Tsuneko had put on the table for him, searching for something. "Ah, here we are. Take this poem, for instance, from the thirtieth poetry party in the second year of Kagen:

> The night sky
> Is moonless, raining;
> Near dawn
> A firefly's light
> Glimmers in the eaves.

"It's an exact description, yet it has an indefinable pathos that effectively conveys the personal sadness underlying the outward splendor of her life. Precisely because she was so sensitive and vulnerable, she rigorously trained herself to conceal her emotions, with the result that these descriptive poems, so emotionally restrained, have a subtle power to suggest feeling. Don't you think so?"

Everything he said, of course, was quite correct; it made it impossible for her to bare her own emotions any further. Yet she couldn't help being aware, at the same time, that something in her mind, some kernel of feeling, had become still firmer. In the end, he had said nothing about the source of the combs. When she thought of the purple wrapping, stored away so carefully in the pocket of the very jacket that he, with such an innocent expression, had given her to carry, and which she on her side, because it was *his* jacket, had held away from her so that it shouldn't get sweat on it as she nearly killed herself struggling up four hundred steps under the blazing sun—when she thought of it, she couldn't stop the feeling from turning into pure resentment. . . .

That evening, nevertheless, nothing untoward happened, and the following morning they set out while it was still cool to visit the Hayatama Shrine. The deity of this shrine—the Professor explained—was generally said to be the god Izanagi-no-mikoto, but according to a passage in the *Chronicles of Japan* it was in fact a god formed from Izanagi's saliva. Saliva, he said, was a symbol of the soul, and the divine spirit in question was intimately connected with burial and services for the dead.

This, together with the loving respect the Professor had shown as he buried the comb, would seem to suggest that the original owner of the combs was no longer alive. Tsuneko, who had been preoccupied with these objects ever since the day before, had had a dream the previous night in which Eifuku Mon'in and the lady of the combs were merged in a dim vision of a woman, a woman no longer of this world yet of unparalleled beauty and nobility. With the three boxwood combs in her hair, her pale, mournful face had loomed out of the depths of the Kumano cedar woods, the train of her robe stretching on and on like the night, trailing far behind her and away into the dark sky. The precise nature of the garment wasn't clear, but Tsuneko must have pictured Eifuku Mon'in wearing something similar. At its neck, fabrics lay in multiple layers from which the face rose like a wan moon. Suddenly, she realized that the many layers were all of white, patterned silk; and at that moment, day began slowly to dawn and the robe, its color revealed as the plain purple of mourning, took on a progressively richer hue.

Of course—the purple wrapping cloth! she thought; and the dream vanished.

She was to encounter the cloth again that morning in the inner garden of the Hayatama Shrine. Here, in contrast to the other site, the precincts were appallingly noisy, the crimson buildings reverberating incessantly with the din, like that of power saws at a lumber mill, made by steamers setting off up the Kumano River behind the shrine.

As a result, the Professor's secret undertaking was accomplished, under the cover of noise, more easily than at Nachi, and the comb with its character *yo*, once taken from the purple wrapping, was buried among the roots of a shrub in no time at all.

That left the one inscribed with *ko*.

Folding the remaining comb tenderly in the cloth, the Professor thrust it deep into the inside pocket of his jacket, then, again without saying a word and without a glance at Tsuneko's inquiring expression, turned a weary, sloping-shouldered back on her and led the way out of the garden.

6

The interest that Professor Fujimiya took in Eifuku Mon'in was inspired not by her verse alone, but also by the fact that the age of the *Gyokuyoshu* was a crucial one in the history of the "Kokin mysteries."

The authority of the Kokin tradition had originally derived from a political struggle. In the antagonism between the Kyogoku and Nijo schools of poets that accompanied the splitting of the imperial line into two rival courts, the Nijo school, as a means of demonstrating its own long-established authority at the expense of the newer Kyogoku school, had gradually begun to present the tradition—till then of no particular substance—as something of great profundity. From then on the original rivalry had, as witnessed by the celebrated *Petitions by Two Nobles of the Enkei Era*, degenerated into the naked expression of a hatred and jealousy that concealed in turn an underlying struggle for political power and wealth. These facts of history Tsuneko knew herself from having been allowed a humble place at the Professor's tutorials.

Two members of the Mikohidari family, which claimed descent from the Kokin poet Michinaga—Tameyo of the Nijo school and Tamekane of the Kyogoku school—were at daggers drawn. Angered by the appointment of Tamekane as sole compiler of a projected imperial anthology, Tameyo appealed to the emperor to disqualify his relative, while the latter on his side made a counter appeal. These were the aforementioned *Petitions by Two Nobles*. Despite this, Tamekane hastened to compile the *Gyokuyoshu* on his own. One of the chief poets represented in it was, of course, Eifuku Mon'in. The struggle eventually ended in victory for the Nijo school and the consequent emergence in its definitive form of the Kokin secret tradition. Professor Fujimiya's studies thus naturally centered on this Nijo school—yet personally he was unquestionably sympathetic to the losing side.

There was no telling what, in the first place, might have touched off his interest in such things: a squalid struggle in a bygone court, and a mystic authority forged by main force. One thing certain was that there were also two conflicting elements

196

in his own personality. While sympathizing with the Kyogoku school in its decline, he worked hard to acquire an increasingly mystic stature of his own; and while devoting his life to studies suggesting that most academic and artistic disputes involved the simple pursuit of self-interest, he was himself an artist, the author of a large number of graceful, poignant poems.

Thus, while Tsuneko was deeply impressed by the Professor's persistence in handling objects that emitted the strange radioactivity known as beauty, to the point where he was weirdly transformed by exposure to it, she could only conclude that to do the same was completely beyond her own abilities. Quite possibly, that was what had given him such an unusually solitary, chilly personality—the suspicion that the beauty distilled from the ugly struggles provoked by man's greed appeared, not on the victorious side but more stealthily, amongst those who were defeated or doomed to extinction; whereas he personally, hoping to establish (albeit in provisional form) his own lasting authority, disliked any hint of such extinction.

In this way Tsuneko, growing calmer, found herself able to take another, less urgent look at him. But remembering that she was going to have to face the purple cloth again that afternoon, she didn't feel up to pursuing the subject.

The Nimasu Shrine, the focal point of the three holy sites, is said to have been established as early as the reign of the emperor Sujin, and the god worshiped there is Ketsumiko-no-kami, the same as at the Kumano sub-shrine at Ou, in the province of Izumo.

According to the Professor's account, Nimasu still showed the lingering influence of the shamanism of the Izumo people. In fact, the religious practices of all the Kumano shrines betrayed strong traces of ideas differing from those proper to esoteric

Buddhism, which gave them a flavor not found in other Shugen-do rites.

There was a bus they could have taken, but to Tsuneko's relief the Professor, who was not mean with money when traveling, said he would hire an air-conditioned car again.

Unfortunately, the drive along the Kumano River followed a rough, stony road on which they repeatedly encountered trucks loaded with timber. Each time, they were enveloped in swirling clouds of dust, so that although the windows were closed with the air conditioning on, it was impossible to enjoy at leisure the view of the river below.

The original shrine had once stood in the middle of the Otonashi River, and had been of great magnificence, but it was destroyed by floods in 1889 and rebuilt two years later on its present site by this river. There were various waterfalls on the far bank, but particularly memorable for Tsuneko was seeing one called Shirami-no-Taki, an offshoot of the Nachi Falls spilling from the rear of the main cascade, which the Professor felt it worth stopping the car to view.

In fact, even though it was refreshing to see the trees and grass round about damp and glossy where everywhere else was white with the dust thrown up by the trucks, it proved to be a perfectly ordinary waterfall. Still, the idea that this was pure, holy water emerging from behind the huge Nachi Falls itself gave the single thread, dropping from the sky as she looked up at it, its own distinction. It occurred to her that, thanks to her companion, she had been allowed to get thoroughly acquainted with every aspect of Nachi: the distant view of it from the sea the day before, then the spray falling on them as they stood by its basin, and today this glimpse of a hidden self, in the background. . . .

Eventually they reached the parting point of the rivers, then followed the Kumano further to the west, over hill and through dale, passing by the Yunomine hot-spring resort, until, just as the wide basin of the Otonashi, a tributary, spread out before them, a graceful shrine building appeared beside the river in a grove of trees.

As she got out of the car, Tsuneko marveled at the beauty of the surrounding hills wrapped in summer sunlight. There were few people about; the clear air was redolent of cedar; and the muddle of the modern world just beyond only conferred a strange plausibility on the traditional belief that this was the paradise of Amida. Even the cry of the cicadas, out of sight in the cedars, had none of its usual shrillness but was still and pervasive, like a fine sheet of bronze foil overlying everything.

Passing beneath the massive, finely proportioned gateway of unpainted wood, they walked slowly along the white gravel of the approach to the shrine, between an avenue of cedars whose foliage grew thick right down to the lowest branches. Seen from the foot of the stone steps leading to the shrine itself, the sky was enclosed in a uniform green, broken only by the touch of a sunbeam on the upper part of a trunk, or a cluster of dun-colored dead needles.

Halfway up the steps, a quotation from the Noh play *Makiginu*, inscribed on a wooden signboard, reminded Tsuneko of the old story.

"It's about a man from the capital who comes here to offer up a thousand rolls of silk, isn't it?" she said.

"That's right. He comes at the command of the emperor, who has had a vision in his sleep. But on the way the man sees some winter-flowering plum blossom, which inspires him to write a poem as an offering to the god Tenjin of Otonashi. As a result, he's late arriving at the shrine and is seized and bound, but is rescued by the god personally, manifesting himself in the form of a shrine maiden . . ."

199

"Who extols the virtues of verse. . . ."

"Exactly. Singing the praises of Buddhism in terms of poetry."

As Tsuneko remembered it, the play had included the lines "The Shojoden enshrines / The Buddha Amida," which suggested the dead, and also: "Ply, ply the comb / On the disheveled hair. . . ," but she refrained from mentioning them because she didn't want to give the impression of being preoccupied with death and combs.

By the side of the steps as they climbed, they noticed a moss-covered stone pillar said to have been set up by Izumi Shikibu. Then, as they reached the top and emerged onto the broad, open space before the shrine, they saw the great bronze knobs that had once topped the railings of the bridge over the Otonashi River, casting strong shadows on the earth on either side of the graveled path that lay white and hushed beneath the afternoon sun.

The entrance had its bamboo blind, red and white with black tassels, rolled up to reveal the interior, but the Professor, giving it no more than a glance, made straight for the shrine office, whence a priest took him and Tsuneko into the inner garden.

There are times when things conspire to thwart: the priest here, who never left their side for a moment, was young and an admirer, it seemed, of the Professor's writings. He began talking about *Flowers and Birds* and showed no sign of stopping. The Professor listened civilly and answered suitably, but his inward impatience conveyed itself quite clearly to Tsuneko. He was eager to be rid of the priest, so that he could bury the third comb.

Noticing him becoming increasingly terse, his responses increasingly reluctant, she had a strong sense of how important the task in hand must be to him, and of how long he must have worked to ensure its success. For such a great scholar to be so obsessed with something seemingly so frivolous implied a correspondingly weighty reason. Reluctantly, the thought rose in her mind, romantic and wistful at the same time, of how beautiful the girl Kayoko must have been; and she found herself wanting to help the Professor achieve his dearest wish.

Thus Tsuneko made up her mind that it was time for her to interfere just once more on this journey. Catching the priest's eye, she drew him to one side.

"Perhaps I shouldn't mention it," she said, "but the Professor always says that he likes to pray quietly by himself when he visits a shrine garden. Although I'm supposed to be his companion on this trip, I think perhaps I'll excuse myself for a while. Don't you think that's best?"

No one could ignore such a broad hint: the priest followed Tsuneko out, and as they went she didn't fail to notice the quick look of gratitude that the Professor gave her from behind his mauve spectacles.

Outside, in the shade of the outer building's broad eaves, Tsuneko waited with a pounding heart. Never, she felt, had she looked forward to his return with more emotion. Almost unawares, she had come to hope and pray that the Professor's three combs would be laid successfully to rest, one in each of the three inner gardens of the Kumano shrines. One reason why she could await him now with such freedom from jealousy or grief—with such happiness, even—might have been that the other woman, however beautiful, was almost certainly no longer living, while her own wanderings through this deep green world of the dead had disposed her by now to forgive its inhabitants their trespasses.

Before long, the sight of the Professor emerging from a side gate in the distance, busily wiping his fingers with a cotton pad, informed her that things had gone successfully. In the sunlight, the floss at his fingertips shone pure white like the flowers of the sacred *sakaki* tree. . . .

It was as the Professor—having firmly refused the shrine office's offer to serve him tea—was sitting in a deserted tea shop to one side of the forecourt, sipping a glass of what was described as "Holy Kumano Water," that he told Tsuneko the history of the combs.

She listened with solemn attention, though the Professor himself related the story, not in the self-conscious, hesitating manner one would have expected with such a tale, but with the characteristic flat delivery that he adopted for his lectures on the romances of the Heian period.

It began with an account of why he had always shunned his home village. This was due, apparently, to its associations with the sad story of a certain woman.

Before coming up to college in Tokyo, the Professor had loved and been loved by a girl called Kayoko, but their parents had broken up the relationship. The Professor had gone away to study, and Kayoko had fallen ill and died only shortly afterward. It had been, he explained incidentally, an illness brought about by the sorrow of frustrated love.

So it was out of respect for Kayoko's memory that he had remained single all his life; and throughout everything he had borne in mind a vow he had made to the girl.

Kayoko had expressed a wish that they should go together on a pilgrimage to the three shrines of Kumano. But the idea of their going on a trip alone together was unthinkable, while marriage was impossible because of family opposition. So the young Professor had declared, disguising his true feelings with a joke:

"Right. I'll take you there when I'm sixty!"

And now he had reached sixty, and had come here to visit the shrines of Kumano, bearing the three combs that symbolized Kayoko. . . .

As the narrative drew to a close, Tsuneko was struck by its beauty. At last, she felt, the secrets of the Professor's solitary life and his deep sadness had been explained. Or rather, she felt this for a moment: for almost simultaneously she had a sense that the mystery surrounding the Professor had, in fact, only deepened, that the story was just *too* beautiful to carry real conviction. The strongest proof of this was that suddenly, as though an evil spirit had been exorcised, no trace of lingering jealousy or uneasiness remained. Nor was she surprised to find herself listening to his story in a completely normal frame of mind, absorbed in the narrative as such.

For the first time, the feminine intuition that she had never trusted before came into vigorous play, alerting her to an element of fantasy in the tale. Yes: from first to last, it should be taken as fiction. If so, then the commitment to this fantasy that the Professor had believed in until the age of sixty, and that had been fulfilled with the burial of the three combs, was something quite astonishing—in a way, a fragile and romantic metaphor of his whole life's work.

And yet—Tsuneko's sense of smell, suddenly sharpened by the last two days' journey, was sniffing out something further still—surely it wasn't even a fantasy? Wasn't the real truth that for some extraordinary reason the Professor, without the least faith in this ritual of burying the three combs, much less the fantasy as a whole, had sought to create, toward the close of his lonely life, a legend about himself?

As a legend, it might seem trite and sentimental; but if that was the kind of thing he liked, it couldn't be helped. With a start of conviction Tsuneko realized, inevitably, that she had hit the mark.

She had been chosen to be the witness.

If it weren't so, why should the tale he had told with such sorrow seem so ill-suited to him? Why should his walleye, his soprano voice, his dyed hair, his baggy trousers, everything about him, give the lie so strongly to the story? One rule that life had taught Tsuneko was that the only things that happened to a person were those that were appropriate to him; the rule had applied with great accuracy to herself, and there was no reason why it shouldn't also apply to the Professor.

At this point, she made a firm resolution on one thing: that from the moment of hearing the story until her dying day she would never betray, whether in front of the Professor or other people, the least sign of not believing it. That was the only logical outcome of the years of loyal service she had given him. At the same time, there arose in her an overwhelming sense of relief; it was as though the despair she had felt the previous day as she looked into the mirror had been cured, leaving no trace of a shadow. From now on, the Professor and she would live in her heart as they really were. Like the character in *Makiginu* who was tied up as a punishment for his preoccupation with poetry, Tsuneko had been released from her bonds by the spirit of Kumano.

"This young lady, Kayoko—," she said, breaking the silence in case, too prolonged, it should seem odd, "she must have been awfully pretty."

The cold holy water remaining in the glass he held was clear and still, as though turned to transparent crystal.

"Yes, she was beautiful. More beautiful than any other woman I've met in my life."

204

Through his mauve spectacles the Professor directed a dreamy look at the midday sky; but nothing he said could hurt Tsuneko any more.

"I'm sure she was—very beautiful. I can almost imagine what she was like from those three combs."

"Lovely as the day. A vision—you should try making a poem out of it," said the Professor. And Tsuneko, radiant, replied:

"Yes, I certainly will."